White Pebbles in the Dark Forests

WHITE PEBBLES IN THE DARK FORESTS

Jovette Marchessault

Translated by Yvonne M. Klein

Talonbooks • Vancouver • 1990

copyright © 1990 Jovette Marchessault

translation © 1990 Yvonne M. Klein

published with the assistance of the Canada Council

Talonbooks
201/1019 East Cordova Street
Vancouver, British Columbia
Canada, V6A 1M8

Typeset in Bem by Piéce de Résistance Ltée. Printed and bound in Canada by Hignell Printing Ltd.

Printed in Canada.

First printing August 1990.

Canadian Cataloguing in Publication Data

Marchessault, Jovette, 1938-
 [Des cailloux blancs pour les forêts obscures. English]
 White Pebbles in the dark forests

 Translation of: Des cailloux blancs pour les forêts obscures
 ISBN 0-88922-280-0

 I. Title II. Title: Des cailloux blancs pour les for-88-ts obscures. English.
 PS8576.A635D413 1990   C843'.54   C90-091224-3
 PQ3919.2.M37D413 1990

To Mary Meigs

First Song
The Serenity of the Snows

I turn toward Noria who is standing in front of the broad window. She has pressed her forehead against the glass and is looking outside as if she were drawn in all her beauty and vitality toward some irresistible someone or something which is coming into existence out there, which is beginning a dance of the celestial body with the snow. What she sees spreads a strange, diffuse light across her face.

"The snow is covering the trees and the ground," she says. "We are entering the clouds where something rests which has never been before. Soon every track will disappear and everything will begin afresh, with an unselfish love. It is both clear and inexplicable," she adds.

We live at the beginning of a path which snakes its way through a broad landscape of mountains, gloomy ravines, waterfalls, ponds, lakes, and so, so much human effort to keep at bay the solitude, the phantoms, and anything else that might fall from the fabric of the night. This path is now a part of the long highway which runs through our existence.

In the Appalachian Mountains, it is the season when the sky is a maritime sky. The winds among the zones of frozen water, sunshine, snowstorms, the Northern lights, the blue sky and the sky before a deep frost when it becomes the colour of a mussel shell, these all alternate with enormous rapidity. Every year I feel the same emotion once again—the more I immerse myself in winter, in the celestial heart of the snow, the more I have the sense that the radiant faces of the universe are descending upon the earth. They bed down on the mountains and in the ponds as if in their own reflections, their muzzles stretched toward the forests of New England . . . of the New Atlantis.

Even if I have been keeping my eyes fixed on this landscape for a long time, it always makes me dizzy, a feeling which grows ever stronger. I know this sensation is a warning from the damned souls, but I can defend myself! Against the dizziness, I take up my defensive (or perhaps offensive) weaponry of questions, of pain, and, as often as I can, of writing. I want to make a point of telling you that the pages which follow are the fruit of a long and slow process of understanding. I can put that another way—that I am confronting the judgement of my own conscience as I remember everything I have done since the moment I was incarnated on this earth. And I, this feeble creature, afraid of everything though I am, I have just recalled that my part, a part which I have by heart but which I had forgotten in the depths of my childhood, my part, I say, is to save the world. As is yours! I am convinced that each and every one of us knows this part . . . even if we try to distract ourselves away from it, to shed it forever through other kinds of marvellous performances, or through dreams of revenge or happiness or glory. Our role is to save this world, so old, so beautiful, so cruel, and so tender, this world which we have loved throughout our numberless generations—our generations of artists and visionaries, of saints and torturers. This old world which persists in each of our births, like a eternal memory. This old world, source of our energy. This old world, whose true nature is the sole desire to shape humanity itself from each child of the earth.

And that instant of Incarnation! That instant of supreme brilliance—in each of our acts of love or generosity, we resurrect its memory in ourselves. Incarnation. I leave the pond. We stride across the first visible earthly realm. We walk on stones while embracing terrifying quantities of sadness and nostalgia. I am carrying my house on my back. No, no, don't look . . . it looks too much like a smouldering pyre. And all the Mothers who are pushing us in the small of the back—they are very, very close, floating on their backs on the river of the dead. Or face to face, up to their ears in the ether.

And what about the Fathers?

The Fathers are a part of this grilling I am subjecting myself to, this terrible and tragic interrogation which we impose on each other mutually and continually, either silently or raucously, like a professional heckler. As if it was our own fault that our courage is ebbing. As if it was our own fault that the ability to draw meaning from the events which are the warp and woof of our lives is dying of inanition. A famine right here. It comes from swallowing all the clichés and clippings, the heady steam of grants, the metallic frenzy, the whole sound of America.

The Fathers? Every time I ask myself this question, I lose the power to express myself for a moment . . . the power to produce that mental and verbal energy which proves that one is still alive. The Fathers? I am up against a wall, and I hear so much weeping. And I hear the sound of all those things that have been worn away by those tears. And I hear that violent theft which was committed so long ago. The years, the centuries, the mounting mass of misery . . . confronted with it all, I feel simple minded. And all one has with which to reveal the approach of a supernatural event is a poor little language, just barely created.

The Fathers are far away. They live on the side of a mountain which disappears into the invisible realm. It's a test. Those who have seen them say that the Fathers travel only by night along the ribbons of stars which look like railway tracks. They say they whistle like steam engines. But this noise could just as easily be the great immortal chord sounded by all the winds together. When they pass in their golden trajectories, the dwellings made of scales, of feathers, of wool, and human skin tremble. It is a vision which splits me in two, me, a lesbian in the twentieth century.

Sometimes I tell myself that it is pointless to try to tell this story. I do not have enough strength for this work. And anyway, does literature have the right to get involved with miracles? Literature, with its critical violence and its need for rational, historical proofs, which it loves to heap up and stir till it makes you sick to your stomach. Writing is like waving a sword in the air, like having a fit of hysterics in the belly of a carp. But all the same . . . if only once literature could think beyond its permitted limits. After all, it is a vocation which persists in walking alone, without leaving the slightest genetic trace. May it come to resemble an enchanting fairy, all moist, who bends above our cradles, hand in hand with the solar angels and the other manufacturers of living form. After all, literature is a Mother, a vital energy which pours itself out into the world. Oh, Mother Literature, I implore you, I beg you on bended knees to protect your little girl on these sterile plains which extend from book to book, these steppes which are increasingly dangerous to cross.

I push away the typewriter, the pages, my coffee cup.

"Literature invariably brings you to the brink of tears," Noria says. "There's no point in crying and being afraid. Come see, it's snowing!"

I have come to stand at the window as well, in order to get close to her body which is the chief source of heat in this chilly house.

"What are you thinking about?"

"I am thinking about desire."

"Today passion faces out onto the snow," she says. "Now what are you thinking?"

"I feel as though I had never understood or seen or dared anything before. I feel as though the city had nibbled away at my perceptions, little by little, starting with my head. The city attacked my courage, my boldness, my capacity to see clearly. What little it left me was only enough to make me reproach myself for wasting my time and that of everyone else while I wandered through the corridors of streets. The telephone alarm signals, the music in the lesbian bars, the harshness and violence of verbal exchanges . . . it all sounded like the crackle of gunfire. I was dead but everyone else still lived, it seemed to me."

"Where did you live?"

"In Montreal, I lived in a small literary reputation for the most part, only interesting to those concerned," I say, laughing. "And each reputation, large or small, is situated in turn on a literary continent. This literary continent irresistibly suggests a mining town. There they work, digging their holes, bellowing the name of their claim and their rights of ownership. These iron moles burrow into the mine, digging themselves in with their picks and shovels and teeth.

"One day, as I was fiercely digging my hole along with the others, my pick shattered the almost mummified corpse of a writer we had all forgotten a long time ago—I had struck it right in the middle of the chest. He had been reported missing. Even if the passage of time and total oblivion had reduced him to the merest skin and bone, I recognized the stink of corruption. I identified the growing, soon to be permanent, atoms of my future. I was swept out of that mining town with the force of an explosion."

"How phenomenal life is!" Noria says.

"Life still terrifies me."

Noria turns toward the big window. She gives a friendly wave to the two dogs who are running about outside, so happy, so happy to be buried chest deep in that white intoxication. They are dancing in the dust of a cloud which must have exploded in the current of the night just above New England, before navigating along the dorsal fin of the Green Mountains.

"Look at them! Look at them!"

Noria speaks with her nose glued to the window so that she can draw closer to the dogs who are running through the avenues of the world.

"Do you know what that is?" she asks, smiling.

I shake my head.

"I don't know anything," I say. "I only know how to do one thing and that is to tremble when I hear the outside door opening."

"Our dogs are progressing along the road of perfection," Noria says. "And they inspire each other on the way! Why are you giving me that incredulous look? These animals come as close to holiness as my mind can conceive it. Dogs, like all animals, are superbly noble. Besides, in all of human memory, has anyone ever come across a vulgar animal? Every beast looks like . . . God," she adds, after a second's hesitation. "Or, maybe, like the mind, because the deepest mind presided over the creation of every living form and so created an infernal jealousy in the human race. We like to say that dogs are submissive, spineless, and stupid animals, lacking spirit and intelligence. As if the current of life, the vital force of both animals and humans, did not flow from the heart's depths. The resemblance between animals and the divine is so outrageously evident that most of us find it quite simply unbearable," she says, so gently, so quietly that my heart breaks.

Noria and her dogs—what dancing, games, hugging and kissing, salvoes of barking, all articulating words of perpetual adoration, spoken in a ringing language which fell over them like a shower of petals from a flower. One would have had to be blind not to see that Only One-Eye, the little Pekinese, and Rimouski-Belle, the collie, idolized Noria. *Rimouski* is a word from the Montagnais language which, according to Noria, can be roughly translated as *dog house*. The two dogs danced around Noria with that internal bubbling, as only birds know how to dance when they have achieved bliss.

"What kind of death do you wish for?" Noria asks abruptly.

"I don't know. I cultivate my atoms, my desires, and everything I am made of."

And I begin to cry without restraint, without even hiding my face in my hands as every human being naturally does. Except, of course, for the very young who have not yet been betrayed. Then the pain inexplicably leaves me, as happens to all creatures who feel, even for a brief moment, at one with their destinies.

"I don't know how I am going to die," I say. "All I know is that I hope you are with me when it happens."

"Death is phenomenal, too!"

"Death merely brushes us like a wisp of smoke."

"Living is a commonplace greatness," she says, catching fire. "We stretch and stretch through the whole length of spring and dance with the good weather that comes with summer. But one day, we begin to view autumn as the enemy. We become depressed and sleepless and notice a pause in that location where, as we begin to understand, the circulation is controlled—everyone must pay the fare. Then the breath fails and the arteries and the heart shut down. It is not on account of illness . . ."

"What is it, then?"

"It is a matter of depth, of confidence, of appetite."

"But what about when winter scratches away at our interior surfaces? What about when we just barely avoid terror and become aware that winter is now our true substance?"

Noria is ardent. I see a kind of love for me in her face. In an infinitely slow gesture, she places her arms around my shoulders. But there is a kind of interior paralysis in this gesture as well.

"I will try to be present when you die," she says, concerned.

Of course, there is no question of my believing a word she's just said. But I observe with a certain pleasure that my hunger for her presence can be satisfied with those words. Her vague promise gives me a comfort that is quite sufficient for the moment.

"Death always makes me think of churches," I say, "and of ectoplasm in chasubles, tolling the funeral knell. And of defeat, the dirty glimmer extinguished in the void."

"And you, do you want it all?"

"I do want it all."

"You desire it all!"
"And I draw it all to me."
"Life to the point of suffocation!"
"I am a bottomless pit . . ."
"Of affection," says Noria, laughing. "You want to give everything to everything—is the tree sick? You give. Is the duck lame? You give. Is someone's spirit troubled? You give."

And while she gently makes fun of me, I see something rising in her, which leaves her and brushes me gently before moving in the direction of the big window through which it is about to go. I call out to this thing, and to Noria, "Don't leave! Don't die!"

I see Noria get up, trembling violently. Upright, perfectly immobile, she shouts, "Let me go! Let me go!" Her entire skin is bathed in a rosy light which glazes her with the warmest of colours. At precisely this moment, I know that she is for me.

"You are my sister who cannot be explained!"

"No," she says in a frigid voice, "I am an error which cannot be forgiven."

At the big window, that thing which had left her pauses at the very moment that it is about to melt through the window and disappear into the landscape. It stops, then moves toward us, touching me lightly as it passes with its luminous expanse, then re-enters Noria, sweeping her face with a beam of light.

I have always known that every human being is made of royal stuff and that every day of that tiny bit of time allotted us on earth can be enriched by a new miracle. I see Noria, I do see her, begin her long descent over the earth of the Appalachian trail. Her long descent . . . the longest, the slowest, and certainly the most beautiful. At last she comes to warm herself. She comes to rub her crackling skin against the skin of others.

And in the air I breathe, I see an angel pass . . . the double of all earthly scenes, of all the luminous silt of galaxies, of all human and sidereal passions, the double passes in all its golden-robed beauty and its boreal crown. Beauty, beauty with which we are obsessed, with all the natural nostalgia of that heart which clings with a terrible strength to that double, that Jacob's ladder leading to the starry highway.

I feel sad and defeated in a way I have never known before, as if I have just lost a member of my secret family. Standing before me,

Noria looks at me with that certain expression worn by those beings which come from regions more distant than our own. We sense that they are making an effort to tear themselves away from where they are (but where is that?) and come, with exquisite politeness, to meet us in our own setting; frequently they have the additional tact to imitate our language and the gestures we are accustomed to.

"You are trembling," she says.

She speaks in the most ordinary possible voice, a voice which takes good care of the most shadowy parts of her.

"You're nothing but a coma," I say.

"The only thing I can do for you is listen to you relate your dreams, your obsessive quest for happiness. And watch the snow falling and the wind sliding over the mortal blessing of passing time."

"And love the dogs who progress along the road of perfection," I say.

I no longer know what I want from her. Did I ever know? At the beginning, that is, when Noria first came with her dogs, I wanted her natural grandeur in my life and in my arms, even if I felt in her presence like a little girl at the edge of a dark forest, the kind of forest New England builds above the old guts of its mountains. Those whitely magical mountains with their deep valleys where glowing secrets brew powerful crises before showing their faces to the light. Later, I simply wanted her beside me under the Manitoba maple in front of the house. The tree of the hundred thousand joys of growing old together. But now we are at another time in our lives—a time of winter and vague fear.

"There is courage," I say. "That's what keeps us going."

"Courage can just as well produce a fine pile of garbage."

Noria comes to fill her glass. Sometimes she starts drinking before noon. Then she will wander through the house like a tortured soul, stumbling into the furniture, drunker and drunker and desperate in her weakness. On other, perfectly sober, days, she will curl up on the sofa facing the mountains until sunset, doing penance, or meditating, or crying silently. But there are other days too when she reads all my drafts, impatient with the time it takes me to get down on paper the interconnecting lives of my characters.

"Courage," Noria acidly continued, "isn't much different from a punch in the jaw."

"It was courage that got Lindbergh up over the Atlantic. It got Alexandra David-Neél into the mountains of Tibet."

"A fine bunch of dramatic characters! Would we have developed that endurance, that aggression, and especially that longevity, if it was not for death in the end!"

"It's not only the fear of death that keeps us alive."

"What, hope? That uncontrollable shuddering, that morsel of springtime that we manage sometimes to wrest from misery."

"There's more than that," I say. "When you sense, when you know in the depths of your being that you are worth more than All, All that you have been able to accomplish . . ."

"And perhaps all you need would have been a little bit of luck . . . but you don't have the words because circumstance, events, even the limits of your own strength get in your way," she says, with a burning sadness. "And you in particular love that sort of soul. I've noticed that."

"Those individuals stir me particularly. I cannot hear them without being moved by that authentic sorrow. What also keeps us alive is the hunger for what is beautiful and just."

"The desire for the good? For truth? But at the same time we are ferociously egotistical and individualistic. How else do you justify that ineradicable instinct for preservation?"

"That instinct for preservation creates civilizations."

"All civilizations are just plays."

"That's the fiery part," I say. "That's our part, along with love."

"Love? Unfortunately, what we know about love we generally learn from bathroom walls."

"Well, I guess there's nothing left for me except to shuffle off to Buffalo."

"You're too late," she says, making a funny face. "Everything's been published there already. All the nightmares have been inventoried and the abysses clearly labelled. And anyway . . ."

"Anyway?"

"There's the herd," she says in a penetrating voice.

"Well," I say, pretending to be horrified, "if there's the herd, that changes everything. It's so much more appropriate to keep your distance from that, wrapped in the genuine obsessional world of your own personal demons."

"To forget the world and to make the world forget you! In your particular case, that might look like egotism, or worse, indifference," she says with a short laugh.

"But the silence, the light, and the solitude in the mountains are indispensable if I am to write. I try to make my books the way you look at a landscape—from the front and from the rear. Then, you make a leap and enter it. You walk, you run over the mossy soil and stop at last to catch your breath. You fasten your ear to the turf and hear whatever has been galloping into the beyond for so long down there. Then you soar toward the tree tops to pursue another unfolding of the landscape and of your characters, when everything moves from the visible to the invisible, following the shortcuts taken by birds of prey."

Noria has just delicately taken hold of my most recent pages on the table. She is sitting with the work of this past week propped on her knees; she bends over the papers, brings them closer toward her eyes without skipping a single word. I have stage fright! What you write is always a problem to other people. Even if you believe you have wrought your magic in a constructive way, you can produce a terrible disintegrating effect. Even with the best will in the world, you cannot separate the material from other people's feelings. Noria might tell me that I had no right to talk about her past, let alone her future. That I did not have her permission to base my novel on her life, on my own life, or on the life which joined us.

"Is it fictional license or a license to spy?" Noria says. "It's a right that always seems to focus on other people's intimate lives and to answer the siren song of secrets, scandals, and hidden weaknesses. It makes me exist where I do not want to be! It's the devil's work," she adds.

"I need a cigarette," I say.

"Go ahead, smoke," she says, with an edge.

"I'll go outside," I say, taking my parka.

"You'll get a gold star on your forehead," says Noria, starting to read again.

Maybe that would be a good thing, I tell myself as I go outside to light my cigarette.

Suddenly, it is noon in the Appalachians and midnight in Alaska. In San Francisco, the dragon lamps on the Golden Gate are lit; in the same instant, the crackling moon lies on her back above the China Sea, that moon which guided Alexandra David-Neél and Lindbergh. To keep oneself alive. To hear and see the flames' debate without shrinking back. Is there any limit? Any limit to what? To understanding, to living, to writing. Even in total exhaustion, even if everything is ravaged by everything else, the flesh and the bones, the masks and the truth.

I walk around the pond, walking and petting the dogs. Rimouski-Belle and Only One-Eye simultaneously are giving voice to a large number of emotions as if there truly were no limit to what blissful beasts can feel. The pond, with its feeling of eternity, its birch forest pressing down behind. It is pleasant to stay there, without moving, in the peace and beauty of the place, to imagine . . . .

I imagine a fabulous epoch when the royal road of the greatest animals in America—bisons, mammoths, elks, white, black and brown bears, mountain lions, and deer—freely ended at this pond. The dogs are drinking. No, the pond has not yet frozen over. Its liquid structure descends into the depths. It is freighted with sand, earth, slaty crystalline schists, and so much more. Heads tucked under their wings, the geese rest on the pond. They dream and slide slowly over the surface of the water until one of them, shaking off the hypnotic trance, trumpets her Last Judgement cry. HANK! HANK! HANK! The others stir, opening their great wings of clarity, creating a different music with the air that ruffles the thunder of their feathers.

The white of their feathers pierces the eye. Yes, the white. But there is the red in the very bottom of the eye, like a terrible poultice. It doesn't matter if you are worthy and ready to attend this Mystery. I look back at that first morning of winter, just after dawn and the first snow. A red fox, hunted by hoarfrost. It was at the same time a piece of fire and fire itself. Before my very eyes, the fox had swallowed down a white goose. Swallowed her. Bore her off with that speed and strength which get you right where you live because they are the elements of survival itself.

The hypnotic effect of blood on the snow. The blood of a snow goose on the snow. The trail of bloody splotches makes its way inside you of its own accord, without asking your permission. It devoutly asks you to be still, and especially not to yell or be repulsed by it but to bow when entering this House of Death. To bow deeply to see this redness which grows, which gives forth its plenty, which escapes first in drops and then in torrents to pay our debts with its enormous strength.

Beside the pond, with its superb view of the Appalachian expanse, my two feet planted at the root of the ancient royal road, I tell myself that I live at a sacred site, that the Appalachian trail is the glowing sash which decides, on earth, between justice and truth and ignorance and disbelief. The snow sifts down its white peace and I tell myself that I have been crouched too long over my writing while the world around me has continued to make and unmake itself, to grow light and then dark, trying always to infiltrate into what I imagine in my mind.

Even so, even so, I have the feeling I have been passing this writing time in a sacred chamber, in a cavern where no one has lived before me, a place where one can always take refuge in order to choose another destiny.

Words, landscapes, animals, and clouds are my lost children. Thus I have murmured to the geese, the dogs, the pond, to the birch woods, the red fox and to the baby mammoth who takes her first faltering steps down there on the gentle slopes of the royal road.

I open the henhouse door. Back in our house, Noria is reading my work. She is reading the words in single file, just as they were written and as it is best to write them. But wolves also go in single file to thwart the hunters. I would so much like to put strange things in this book—peaceful and well-meaning ghosts, or other mysterious and frightening apparitions which grind their jaws, sepulchral offerings. Or still more terrifying spectres, vengeful, bone-cracking divinities, which loom suddenly with demonic fury from the shadowy depths to give ghastly life to our nights of destruction. At the same time, I do not forget those which come from heaven, leaping from the flame bearing offerings of wheat, of spirits, and of flowers. Noria's arrival at Goose Pond belongs to this order of radiant apparitions. The longer she stays here where she has been tossed up by a strange set of circumstances, the more I feel that a kind of reality previously unknown to me wants to reveal itself.

A gleam of light laps at the depths of the sky. I am afraid. I am managing less and less to repress the suffocating rise of my tears. Depression? Despondency? Too strong an inclination toward mysticism? Hysteria? A fundamental weakness of character? Mental structures of insufficient breadth? I am frequently overcome by an oppressive sense of futility. Is the fear of death of little consequence? Is that final wrenching departure fire-slow or winter-long? The fear of being left behind if your loved one were to die. The regret at leaving behind someone we have barely begun with, someone whom we have loved the most, or those who have been for us witnesses to love and whom we do not know how to repay. What is the verdict?

Entering the henhouse, I frighten the chickens, who stir, displaying a splendour of shimmering feathers. The roosters utter their sentry calls. Picking up a still-warm egg, I mutter to myself that I do not invent the apparitions which I would reveal in my novel—they really exist. From at least the beginning of time, they have run their mad course through our memories, surfacing in everything the human spirit may do to rise out of nothingness to extinguish the fear of death or free itself from suffering.

I think back to the first woman I ever loved, the first I lived with. She was in thrall to a goddess of vengeance whom she invited to our house in the middle of the night. Such a crash, such ritual dancing, beginning with the devilish ritual—the test plummet. When she arrived at her destination, she ran about, surely as terrified as I myself, the captive witness, could be, the floor burning with desperation. "Why don't you leave her? Watch out for yourself. It's masochistic." That's what the choir of my well-intentioned lesbian friends would chant. One of them, who thought she was more perceptive than the others, said, "What are you making yourself pay for?"

But how can you not listen to, not hear, the cries of pain of a woman you love (or those of a man, a child, an animal)? A woman who lays her life bare before you, a woman who is trying to get in contact with whatever is most base in order to confront, in their totality, the destructive fires of the goddess whom she incarnates. Watch. Listen. But do not judge. But remain silent. Above all, remain silent. And any words you might say, even the tenderest and the most sincere, are the wrong words. The mere contact between words and the goddess causes wounds.

Night-time. The departure gate for conspiring souls. Lost identity. the goddess of vengeance wears her ravenous mask, her fangs and claws. Her spear. Her harpoon. To rend, section, overwhelm, and bend above the now-purged corpse. She attacks!

"Your writing is pathetic."

She parades all my crimes and iniquities before my face. I straighten my spine—I am ready and worthy. She showers me with insults; she brings them to me in person—an offering.

She marches up and down in the bounty of her strength.

Silently, I stretch my arms out towards her. She strides around my chair several times, right up to the entrance to hell. I await my sentence. I will be purged among those who have been purged.

"You refuse to evolve. Our relationship is at a total standstill."

The goddess marks a pause. I look directly at her. She fondles her final oracle voluptuously.

"You are nothing but a ghoul. You keep me from living."

The goddess of vengeance picks up the pace. She flaps about. She changes shape, becoming first my mother, then my father. I eat the consecrated bread and drink the nectar of the gods. I grant myself the right of way. We approach the sanctuary. The track of the goddess disappears into a mist of tears and sweat. Frantic, she rotates faster and faster.

"You make me want to go back to fucking men!"

She plants her body firmly in front of me to launch her harpoon.

"This is my house you're in. Get out!"

She opens her door. The true name of this door is a mystery to me. I do not move.

"Out!"

But where will I go in the night? I have no money, no warm clothes, and my shoes have holes in them. I have no songs of jubilation or incense or perfumes. And then, there are my cats. You cannot walk the streets at night with your arms full of frightened cats.

The goddess is about to express herself for the last time. I know it. I am in communion with her. If she does not express herself once more time, she will die, crushed.

"I don't want to see you any more. It's over." She points to the open door, the gloom of the staircase. I do not want to leave, abandoning my cats to the ravening mask. I do not know how to appease the wrath of the vengeful deity. But I feel at peace when I tell her in a calm voice: "I'm staying."

After four years, I am out of jail.

Considerably later, the day and the hour being auspicious and being wholly reunited with the earth and with the lovely order of the stars, I am to meet another goddess. But this one was peaceable and benevolent. Vengeance was altogether absent in her. An old spirit whose life was making great strides. I felt she had been sent to me to teach me many eternal, radiant things. Three years of happiness. I was a peacock, an eagle, a holy cow. I was forever shedding my skin and my new one was volcanic. I was throwing oil on the fire. Together, we lived through all sorts of upheavals. But when we looked each other in the eye, we saw a snowy peace.

I wrote. There was so much material in my life. I was moving in positive circuits equipped with patience and ecstasy. I was purring. I was awaiting favourable atmospheric conditions to find the exact word and the precise harmony. The third year of living together was over when I had this dream—I saw a swarm of bees resting on the lips of the woman I loved. Resting there, making honey, then flying away buzzing, spinning a golden thread which they bore into the heavenly blue, contesting it to the four winds. This dream plunged me into confusion. The bees were rising into the sky, making a noise like thunder and the golden thread was rising into those regions where those no longer in need of wings pause to watch the world turn. I heard the musical cascade of the voices of the children of the earth. That golden thread seemed to me closer to the truth of our lives than all the productions of the critical faculty that works in us. The Medusa may snicker, but this golden thread is speedier in its motion and stronger in its effects than either jealousy or death.

We were going to be separated. Is that the way our lives always come out? After that dream, I never saw the woman I loved with the same eyes. I knew that she had hidden children, children who were peacefully sleeping. One day, she told me in tears, "Yes, it's true, I want children—at least two."

Children with their little gesticulating hands, their golden eyes. Children who will save the world. The will to become flesh must have its perpetual principle in the general atmosphere, in the great, seamless atmosphere, the atmosphere of the family aura.

That's what I told myself as I was packing my suitcase. The cats, motionless, followed me with their eyes. I was leaving them to the benevolent deity. This time, they had found a home.

As I close the door to the henhouse, I say goodbye to the chickens. The dogs are waiting for me, their throats throbbing. They seem to be saying, "Oh, there you are, my friend. We're playing a game that any number can play." Rimouski-Belle makes the first leap, forcing her way into the air. Bravo! Now it's my turn. Not so hot! Only One-Eye amazes us with an almost supernatural leap. What height! We begin all over again, trying to combine deep breathing with our bodily movement. In my case, gravity is an insurmountable obstacle. Rimouski-Belle has developed a technique which allows her to gain extra inches off the ground, but it is Only One-Eye who gets all the cheers. There is just one reasonable explanation—Only One-Eye is a *lung-gom-pa!* That's not surprising since her ancestors guarded the Imperial Palace in Peking in the old days. If you are a *lung-gom-pa,* to walk from Peking to the mountains of Tibet and Lhassa only takes a couple of weeks, or even a few days. Alexandra David-Neél wrote about these *lung-gom-pa* or entranced travellers in the most astonishing pages of her travel account—indifferent to natural obstacles, to the weather, to their own exhaustion, the *lung-gom-pa* progress without stopping for days and days, in order to enter into an expanded condition under the guidance of a spiritual guide from whom they have received a telepathic communication. Likewise, they will undertake long journeys in order to assist their neighbours.

Certainly, the *lung-gom-pa* tear themselves from the earth with every step and bound forward like rubber balls. *Lung-gom* believes that the mind can master matter, the explosions of our nerve cells. All of the exercise leading to *lung-gom* are spiritual in nature. It is said that the sacrifices demanded of the novices are so great that only those endowed with exceptional spiritual qualities can successfully complete the long apprenticeship.

Then again, it is necessary to renounce, to abandon that hysteria which takes possession of the body, to bury it further still in matter, and push it to confront levitation at whatever cost. To renounce too that mad chemistry which impels us to chase after the thunderbolts of glory and mastery. Did I ever renounce ambition and fame? When I told Noria that a explosion had swept me out of the city, was what

I said the truth? Didn't a good pinch of wounded vanity and snivelling narcissism enter into it?

Montreal . . . I lived there buried to my waist in fear. In order to preserve my tiny fame, I did all the right things. What was so fascinating in those cultural circles was that everyone treated everyone else completely equally—that is, as a backdrop, a backdrop for one's own ego. These were the surroundings in which I underwent some devastating personal crises. Often I burrowed inside my armour in order to protect myself. At other times, I lost my footing and plunged into the depths of depression, into the depths of hatred for other people and contempt for myself, as far as I could go into self-pity. Don't touch me! I was a valley of desolation. I was the other and revolting beneath my impeccable exterior. At the same time, I was a great visionary and all they wanted to do was smear me with their shit. Is this wrenching alternation between highs and lows really necessary for us to grow? How can we avoid these dizzying losses of balance, of the balance I believed I would attain with age?

If, despite everything, I rose to the surface, it was because I had clasped to myself that interior light, a single ray of which appeared like those roots which connected me to other people, to my travelling companions along the path. This pilgrimage brings us back to our childhood dreams, since in childhood the heart can only dream that life is a dream. Childhood's heart remains open for a long time to the vision of the enchanted spring. The Great She-Bear and the heavenly constellations come to these surroundings to relate their legend; hearing them in the fullness of our childhood makes us realize that the legend is simply the story of ourselves.

Back in the house, Noria has lit the lamps. It is only noon, but the daylight will not linger for long. Above the Appalachian trail, the dull violet clouds, drifting toward the North, already hide the mountains. I tell Noria about the prodigious strength of the little Pekinese.

"If you were to disappear," I said, "all I'd have to do is put Only One-Eye on a leash and follow her. She would find you anywhere, even beyond the grave."

"And where are you going, may I ask?" said Noria, rattling the pages of my manuscript.

At that moment, I felt like a little blob of jelly trembling on the surface of the universe.

"It's you and my own youth," I said. "I haven't wanted to have a conversation with it for quite a while. Hello, there, friend. And how are you, madame? And your passions? And your family? And your familiars? As always, you are overcome with muteness. But I press on! What have you done to obtain your enchanted gardens? You who have lived for so long a time in those sinister neighbourhoods where they scratch and pinch and fornicate day and night. Dear friend of my youth, I thought you were dead, lying violently murdered in an indifferent world. I want to gain your favour; I want to ornament you richly, make offerings to you, and wash your feet on a sacred stone. In my kingdom, I'll have you know, I never think about you without feeling a hammer beating in my head."

"The kingdom's gone," said Noria. "The real estate agents have made it into condos and parking lots."

"Well, we still have the Andes and Tierra del Fuego."

"And the northern forests and the green mountains. Our task is to consecrate this immense nature and name it Vert-mont, the green mountain, so as to signify that its hills and mountains will be forever green and never vanish."

Noria enunciated these words with fervour. I recognized that same intensity which you encounter when ejaculating a prayer which is rooted in your childhood.

No, these mountains of the New Atlantis will not vanish. They unite us and blend us, attaching the most isolated of human souls to the rest. The mountains of the Appalachian trail are filled with spirits working day and night in the eternal process of becoming. The trail and its Lords of Light—black pines upon red pines toward the giant population of white pines; lower down, larches upon willows upon balsam firs, maples upon oak trees, paper birches upon willows all the way to poplars. Lower yet, toward the clearings, where the land swells and the flat country begins to appear, the houses of the lesbian community. For the community, this is the point of departure and the point of contact for the new era. Under cover or out in the open, the community talks among themselves and tries to prepare the ground before starting work on building another world.

"I've been thinking about your book. I am focusing all my attention on your book," Noria says, in a voice that bodes no good.

"It is only a trip through time," I say. I am avoiding the issue, while pretending to reveal everything.

"A round trip?" Noria asks, pained at my half-truths.

"A round trip for the both of us."

And if she was going to tell me that her return was unlikely . . . I immediately feel a shiver running up my back.

"I am performing an exorcism, Noria . . ."

"An exorcism?"

"You know—Fiction, Fiction, Fiction."

"That's like asking a favour from an enemy," she says in a hostile voice.

"Book or no book, it's all about life and death in a state of profound nervous tension," I say.

"That must be inscribed in your genes. A kind of short in your brain cells. Fiction! For you, fiction seems to be the be-all and end-all of the human species."

I don't answer. If I were in Noria's shoes, I'd be afraid too. Other people's words can diminish us or swallow us whole.

"This book," I say in a voice I hope is reassuring, "seemed to me like a prime opportunity to fill my pages with . . ."

"With the truth—your truth," she says acidly.

"No," I say, "with serenity."

"I had a dream about you," Noria adds bitterly, "I dreamt that you were scouring all the libraries and all the archives to assemble all possible proofs of my lesbianism."

I feel my temples begin to throb and my face grow warmer and warmer.

"Please, please don't talk like that. You know I don't want to hurt you."

"I know," Noria said after a moment. I see her outstretched arms.

"You are a hunted woman."

"You can see that and still you insist!"

"I insist on a community of spirit and heart."

"That's an ultimatum! Surely your patience has some limits?"

"Patience itself has limits. But I know I was wrong in reproaching you in any way."

"You're not wrong," Noria says. "You're the one who does all the nasty jobs no one else wants to touch. I am a coward most of the time."

"You are a soul in absolute despair."

"That is my weakness," Noria says, as if dismissing me.

"It's all my fault," I say frantically. "I ask you to walk before me, lighting the way because I can only mark time in the shadows. Sometimes I have the odd impression that the time we've spent together has lasted only as long as a brief nap. You know, that ephemeral moment just before you fall asleep when you confuse the light from a forgotten bedside lamp with a cloud of shadbush flowers."

"That's Chang-tse's dream," Noria says, putting her arms around me.

She is so sincere that it is impossible for me to hold a grudge. Never. And it's so nice to feel I am loved, even in this way, and despite everything that I am; that is, despite my crass nature, that I take her in my arms as well, truly and eternally.

"One day," Noria continues, "Chang-tse was taking a nap and in a dream saw himself become a butterfly which took flight toward a garden where he bent down for a hundred years before the most beautiful flowers of the realm of dreams before taking a sip. When he awoke, in fact hardly any time had passed and he wondered, 'Should I believe that I am a butterfly in Chang-tse's dream, or Chang-tse in a butterfly's dream?' "

"What does that mean?"

"It means that we live in a world of illusion."

"I too believe in the truth of what appears in dreams, especially if they are fantastical and warn of catastrophes. Anything that can feed my neuroses and self-pity. Probably because I was raised under the sign of the flames of eternal damnation and I have a feeble spirit."

"You!" Noria says serenely. "You have the spirit of a tyrant."

"But I think tyrants were all heavy drinkers. Like you! I'm a teetotaller."

"There's more than one kind of tyrant," Noria says mockingly. "There are those who die young, bending their elbows, and those who live to a hundred or thereabouts, and drink only water."

"If I'm really a tyrant, then there are only two things to do. The first is to call my publisher and demand a big advance. The second, but that is really the first . . ."

"You are as transparent as glass," Noria says. "Your novel, your book . . ."

"My novel about deliverance."

"Your deliverance, to be sure. I remember the first time I came here," Noria says. "Oh, how happy I was to meet a writer. I didn't know yet that I was looking at someone whose primary satellite was her imagination."

"I think you actually were prejudiced," I say.

"As far as you were concerned," she adds tranquilly, "I was already a character in your novel."

"Everything around a writer often enters into her area of expression. I don't deny it."

"Her Noah's Ark."

"That's a nice way to put it. And, speaking of characters in novels, I think I was one in your novel, too."

"Maybe I have an unusual talent for the romantic novel," she says, and smiles.

"What is a writer, anyway? She is someone who is constantly playing around with scenes and she takes her first morning cup of coffee with scraps of sentences shredded in her head. She is someone who walks around in the energy of her world which she talks to, loses patience with, and shatters with a crash. And then she takes time to reframe the page and grow new flesh over whatever was sick or bloodless."

"That must be heady ecstasy—or the devil's work," Noria says with affecting simplicity.

"A novel—it flickers with vital little fires capable of giving birth to great and imperfect things."

"Does a novel happen when the memory of what has been meets the memory of what has not been?" she asks with some concern.

"That's only a step away from it . . ."

"A step you have not hesitated to take! Reading the opening pages of your novel, I thought—I am holding a fiery animal in my two hands," she says with a certain anger.

"And *animal* is the key word of our relationship," I say. "Your enchantment by day, your enchantment by night."

"You're just jealous of the affection I . . ."

"Of the love you have for animals? No, I have come to terms with jealousy."

"Tell me the novel you are making up about it," she says.

"Your love for animals allows me to take intense advantage of every instant you are here. I started to write an entire novel about that from the first months after you came. Every time you left, every time you came back, I wondered, why does she always come back here? I knew that you were not in love with me and that you would never be in love with me. That's the way it was, even though a simple and sometimes disturbing affection glittered from you. I sought a very deep, interior reason that would cause you to come back to Goose Pond, because each time you left, I had to survive the destruction of my world and rid myself of that feeling of sadness which would overwhelm me in your absence. One day, I told myself the following story—Noria comes back on account of her deaths. Why had I not understood that before! She comes back to intone her hymns and say her prayers, and lay her flowers and white pebbles on the graves of all the animals we have buried together along the Appalachian trail. This is how she worships her Great Ancestors. For I have finally understood that in Genesis according to Noria, animals are the Mothers of humanity.

"If you are to approach this Genesis, you must point yourself in the direction of the House which has been illuminated since the beginning of the world. This House loosed its internal organs from the sky a long time ago in order to teach us that the One engenders the Other, for all things must work in concert toward the Advent, toward the splendid innovation of form. Just as, perhaps, the primal reign on earth, so hard, opaque, and underground, in its crystalline, geometric beauty, one day crossed the borders of inertia, coming to life to juggle with the nascent desire for a form distinct from itself. Ravaging its heart, mining its own viscera, it engendered the new forms, forms packed with new possibilities, of the Second Age. This anarchic, oceanic reign took up the challenge and set about inventing mosses, trees, flowers, the ovule, pollen, and the tall meadow grasses of both sea and land, wherein, after aerial dancing and some explosive bursts, it engendered the Third Age.

"The Third Reign, with the same keenness, the same patience, invented swimming, flying, slithering, and wild racing; claws, fangs, and hides, and the burrow, the nest, the egg, and the womb. With its giant belly, solar plexus, and intelligence, the animal reign of the Mothers began, very gently, to imagine us, the human beings, as a possible ideal. And as the previous reigns had likewise done over the millennia, the Third Age would, from a handful of sky, a bit of cloud, a drop of salty water, and a pinch of sand, give us flesh, put the finishing touches to us, and set us down in the promised land."

"And the Fourth Age," Noria says, her voice trembling, "will in its turn begin to invent the future. It dreams of utopias! It delights in adoration and destruction, in cruelty and pity. In its own time, it imagines a possible ideal."

"In several millennia, when we have given rise to the Fifth Age, it will be our turn to be Ancestors. Who knows what this new age will remember of us as it tells its tales and stories to its children . . ."

"I can hear a strange noise," Noria whispers, "It sounds like a noise twisting its roots."

"That's the sound of your blood, my love. If I could explain it to you," I say . . . .

"Love is what you have to explain. Write!"

She goes and presses her forehead against the glass of the big window, crossing the threshold of her life to watch the merciful whiteness falling on the promised land.

Second Song
The Red Cicadas

Lying in my bed in a house swept by every kind of energy, I could not sleep. All night long, inspired by the forces of upheaval and liberation, storm bellows had been raking the length of the mountains and pounding their drums, greeting those divinities who live in a time and space which is not yet our own. And then, at the very moment that I felt that my anxious pursuit of sleep was about to end and I would finally be able to abandon myself to the exquisite opium of oblivion, it was just then that I heard them!

People who have lived a long time in the mountains will tell you that they are the voices of the earth. Others call them the voices of the night and death and are afraid. I believe that it depends on one's vision, one's understanding. It doesn't matter much what names are used, since it seems that very few people hear these voices, so low do they speak beneath the roaring of the prowling winds, in tones which seem to come from the bowels of the earth or the depths of space. If, one day, they should reach you in all their vibratory beauty and distinction, you will hear them clearly since they have a tonal force and an evocative power so great that they are capable of summoning the shadows of entire scenes from your past and future. The scenes which they produce always come in pairs—one seems to blow on the other to make it disappear, so much so that the characters, the sounds, and the colours merge without a break in the continuity.

When I heard these voices clearly pronouncing my name with a smooth and irreversible intonation, I first of all experienced a simple curiosity and turned trustfully in their direction, with even a certain eagerness. Instantly, they made me hear a noise throbbing with superhuman effort, a bubbling which swelled and shrank. It sounded like . . . . Yes, there it was—a throng of canoes ascending the river of air above the mountains, their paddles scraping the peaks. But when I opened my eyes wide, I saw nothing at all! I strained my senses to catch each sound and smell which might be moving through the night close to me. The night seemed thick as felt. A hissing barely perceptible in the silence. I was uneasy and growing impatient. I had a salvo of applause ready in my hands for the flotilla of canoes which ought to have already been in sight. Why had this flotilla not reached me when it *could* reach me? And it was only then that I realized two things at once—that the canoes were not coming and that I, Jeanne, had no body.

It was agonizing now not to have a body. One's own body, a body around oneself. A body with its delicate fibre, its forces of attraction, its magnetic will. A body gone slightly soft, somewhat thick around the middle, but beautiful nonetheless, serviceable, able to make the rounds of my smallness and my size. At that moment, I would have given anything to have a body, any body. One that was epileptic or terribly old and shaky would do. Or dying! I'd even take a dying body, clamp it on my soul, tie up all its atoms, bind up its assorted powers and force longevity upon it. Nor would it last only for a single day. A body, a bloody current, the strongest current in the world.

I heard the voices speaking my name again and tried desperately to take on the contours of the name they pronounced. But it was no good! I wandered through my homeland, revisiting the places where I had lived. I went back to the scenes of my childhood, haunting church porches and accosting strangers. I beg your pardon, sir, madam, but I need a body. They pretended not to see me, not to hear me. What crime had I committed? I spoke to a stray dog who turned ail, howling. I spoke to the rats who disappeared into the walls, terrified.

I decided to concentrate my quest—I turned toward my neighbours, the red cicadas. Among them were writers whose passions were readily engaged, almost-chaste lesbians, mothers who were capable of even greater follies, arrogant intellectuals who were nevertheless enormously clever in managing human affairs, and a provocative mixed-bag of humanists and pacifists. Oh, please, friends, I need a body. Nothing doing. Then I turned to the lady-killing prophets, to the ascetics stuck in their own egos, and to the overworked professional ecologists. Still no luck! I gave up trying to move them. I was dead and no one wept. I could not stand it! I heard the voices crying out to the invisible—"Kill her!" I was seized from behind, torn with the talons of a storm of rain and snow. The earth shook, and the mountains of the Appalachian trail collapsed.

When the voices showed me my corpse, an immense cold filled me. It was winter and my corpse was frozen. It was summer and it was rotting. There was nothing left for me but to stretch out on the bare earth and sleep in the heat of my blood.

"Just show me a hole and I will crawl into it," I said.

With great compassion, the voices told me to bear my sufferings, since they were the fruits of my own actions.

"Who judges me? What sin have I committed?"

"Whom should you ask those questions of if not yourself?"

"I was in the light, attached to particular spot on earth," I said. "Let's return to life, okay? To its enormous vistas."

"Stop looking for a body," they said.

"Don't tell me I'm awake when I know I'm asleep . . ."

"You have not learned to meditate."

"I am suffering too much!"

"Meditate!"

The voices fell silent. Something even more horrible was about to happen to me. They were going to light the spotlights of heaven and judge me.

"You have not learned either prayer or meditation," the voices resumed.

"You have clotted my heart's blood and now you want me to forget my terror and my torment."

"Open yourself. You will be free of all personal preoccupations . . ."

"And then what?"

"You will see at last what was created at the moment you yourself were."

"My double?"

The good genie from the marvellous lamp. I had first encountered it, quivering and throbbing, in my mother's womb; its vibration had spread as if it were the Spirit of the World. Under the glare of the spotlights, standing on a handful of red earth, I was judged by a solar angel. Through my tears I saw my unselfish deeds marked with white pebbles and my hurtful ones with black.

I sank again into a frightful daze. I cried out that this was all a mistake.

"In that case, we will look into the mirror of your deeds," the voices answered.

I shouted that I had not done anything wrong, that I would rather disappear than know.

"Those are absurd lies," the voices said.

I was wrenched from the ground and thrust into the air toward a mountain which loomed above the others. I was flying above the purest of emerald green lakes surrounded by mists which looked like gold dust.

"Here is the site where you will be able to view the mirror of the King of Death. Look at it! This mirror reflects your past actions. You will see them clearly and distinctly."

But who could this violent woman be who was reflected here? I could hear her murmuring that death is a good thing for some people. I saw some people die under the stinging words she showered on them. I saw her taking unfair advantage, mocking weaknesses and sneering at satisfaction. I saw her running about the world feverishly, greedily, in search of truth and never approaching the hidden depths which her vanity kept concealed from her. I saw her shrink from others' sufferings and offer them only a deaf ear or an overburdened shoulder. I saw her self-pityingly haul out her handkerchief to mop at a perpetual cold.

I heard her staining the earth, the air, the water, and all living beings with her constant, insatiable, physical, sexual demands. And with her lascivious curiosity, her rapacity. I saw her making illness a form of essential activity—self-intoxicated by her passions, her emotions, her rebelliousness, she was interested only in herself and was so irritable that she suffered from a chronic inflammation of her little ego.

If someone wounded my pride, I tried to take my immediate revenge, by making progress in my work, crushing some and excluding others. And if I couldn't do it quickly enough, I succumbed to bitterness and frustration.

In the mirror of my actions, I saw myself in all my various mutations—from rubbish to rot, an inexhaustible fertility. What could I do? Throw myself at the mirror and try to reduce it to bits? But I'd already done that! Like a punchdrunk fighter who gets a charge out of being hit and seeing his own blood flow. Hacked into pieces by the shards of mirror, I now saw myself in all my facets. Quick, give me an alibi . . . .

"I was born to a slave mother and father," I told the voices. "My parents inhabited imaginary cathedrals of religion and culture. They dedicated those factories to producing monsters which were admired by all."

"That does not excuse you," said the voices. "Your parents are your own choice."

I caved in.

"Do not be afraid," said the voices once again, "when the white pebbles and the black are counted . . . Close your eyes . . ."

When I opened my eyes, it was to hear the song of my dear little black-capped chickadees. Their chick-a-dee-dee-dee was articulated so clearly in the long pause of time. From then on, this song would come to me from as far away as the distressed souls of all those who had died in my dream. I leapt up to throw myself toward the window—and there were all my wild birds in the silver maple. Grasping the trunk, the very image of that overwhelming force which anchors us in matter, the slightly mocking hairy woodpecker tirelessly crackled his own identity—pic, pic, pic. The jays moved about as if a wild wind was blowing or as if they were sliding noisily along azure-slicked rails of air. Wandering grosbeaks, their flight undulating and resonant, went from the silver maple to the Manitoba maple and the purple finches alighted and uttered their rapid call, bending their heads time after time toward the snow, looking for a good-weather truce and fluffing up their raspberry-coloured feathers.

It was a fair and very cold winter morning, one of those mornings when the only thing to do is to get up and say yes to everything. To everything! Fear and the smoky grime of the past are swept away. You can still picture the golden chariot of the Great Bear racing toward the north. I got dressed, went outside, and put out some food for the birds. Then I went off to the edge of the pond to watch them swoop down on the food, wave after wave, shining spirits, devas, oracles, messengers, companions, and guides to the beyond, key of dreams, heraldry, portents, and in their throats the song of those who are only passing through. And human memory recalls that the throats of birds also contain the first articulate language which we were taught.

Something swells and opens in the human body when the birds take flight, pushing away the earth from their feet and bearing our food toward the sky. Oh, you have only to stretch out your hand to pick up one of these starry feathers. The ethereal and telepathic matter of which birds are made seems to me to be appropriate for the revelation of secrets.

I turned my gaze toward the south. The sky still uncoiled clouds of snow showers and further off, I could make out the dance of smoke above the chimneys and houses of the lesbian community. The red cicadas! That is the name I privately give those distant neighbours, inspired by the gigantic cicadas of the Malaysian rain forest. These are bigger and have a broader wingspan than flycatchers or chickadees. They are at least as big as the purple martin. They are definitely the queens of their realm.

It is only after they have, like all cicadas, remained in the earth for seventeen years, among the minerals and roots, that they finally rise from their caskets of earth into the air to chirp out their torrid song which they have been incubating for so long in humus and obscurity. Is it this long sentence in the earth which gives such spirit to their song? There is, so it seems, a quiet rumour about which attributes to this song an aphrodisiac effect.

Among the red cicadas, there are some lesbians who have an old tinge of the Catholic about them. There are others who, even if they never take part in the rituals and observances, say they are connected to Protestantism or Judaism. And then there are others who, committed pagans or atheists, prefer to savour the strange sensual pleasures of radicalism or the most intolerant kind of separatism. No salvation outside the lesbian people! No pleasure outside the nation of lovers!

What is so amazing about the atheists and the separatists is how they seem to have borrowed from the "man's world" some religious observances regulated by ritual—they show off their leather, suede, and tweed jackets, their regular ties or their bow ties, their army boots, their short hair, and their aftershave lotion. They are our female knights, these diesel dykes of North America. Our female knights like to travel across the continent looking for adventures with women. Off they go, astride the docile mares of their lively string, brandishing the flaming sword of autonomy. With their tough expression and tougher muscles, their faintly faunlike attitude, seeking fame through an ancient lineage, they enjoy making the labyris, that double-bladed axe of Amazon legend, whistle through the air while singing in serious voices all the words of the witches' revolution, like music borne upon the wind.

But when they get down off their high horses, stop fighting with unreality, and quit telling us what we ought to think, they succumb, as we do, to the incantatory song of all vegetable matter in the lovely summer nights along the Appalachian trail. Especially to those herbs devoted to the human spirit which are transmuted into narcotic beverages and healing balms to cure our life-pain and inspire us to adopt another mode of life. Alas, the transmutation of vegetable matter is fraught with far fewer difficulties than is the transmutation of human beings.

Our female knights always talked about lesbianism as a means to freedom and emancipation.

"A window opening on the world?" the nonbelievers asked ironically.

"A window which holds as much of earth as the sky and the sea," the female knights replied. "A kind of back-flow, a rising tide which comes up through time—the linked chain of ancestresses."

I thought, as did a lot of others, that the predictions of the female knights would find their roots in the universal ideal of the superman. Only this time, it was a question of the superwoman, Mother, Goddess, primordial entity whose beloved children we were, without regard to race and gender, since humanity is nourished at the same living source!

"We summon woman souls, founders, writers of memoirs," the female knights said drunkenly. "And because we dream of beauty, we are patrons of the arts."

When they unrolled their imaginings this way before us, I was certain that they did it not to mislead but to enchant us. Furthermore, I came to dream with them that once upon a time, long ago, we were free of our acts. We could, as we chose, traverse the earth, the sky, the sea, sail toward the stars in solar barques, and visit worlds beyond our world, since once upon a time our spirit commanded a vertebrate body better than our present one.

I do not remember from what corner of the ancient world these often chaotic images reverberated, these proud affirmations, these manifestations of fear, of disgust, and pain. But behind the mask in the depths of each woman, in what it was that made us all banished women, the simplest among us came to terms with experienced suffering, feelings of helplessness, and love tainted by the abject voice of humiliation.

In the light of this ancient past, a number of lesbians were convinced that they embodied an emotional crisis because of a wild confrontation with invaders, with the brutality of conquest. When intoxicated by a fantasy of glory and triumph, our priestesses and spiritual guides begged a propitiatory offering, and we would always agree to pay our tithes in blood. Raised in the surety of a return to the land of the Great Ancestors in the shape of the South Wind or of a Bird of Paradise, we would enter death as one might begin to dance.

In another time, I remember that we walked along a road burnt by the sun. Chained to our companions, we understood that the people looked on us as if we were hunting trophies.

On another occasion, we were bound to trees and, not permitted the tiniest gesture to defend ourselves, handed over to mad dogs to entertain the populace.

I kept a very particular memento from this last scene—I raked the earth with my nails to dig up some cancerous mummies which I happily stripped of their jewellery and golden teeth. Motionless, the very image of a silent and imposing Beyond, a scarab with fiery eyes looked at me, Jeanne, crouching down, enriched with his ceremonial phallus.

These memories of episodes in my past beset me with extraordinary violence. These memories . . . . It was as if great, well-oiled machines of war, brimming with fuel, were primarily occupied with furrowing my consciousness with their wild acceleration along straight lines, their squeals, their puffing in the turns and up the grades. I could hear their howls of pleasure each time I remembered, with the precision of hallucination, certain acts undertaken in the spirit of revenge. Some of these acts were performed collectively and others individually. Little by little, I began to make out the splendours of truth, the burning imprints of what I had thought I had forgotten, standing out on a piece of untanned leather.

Who has hidden that peeled skin which blisters and cracks with a hiss under the effects of heat? See it tearing itself apart to the end of the world and offering us its tender cheek made of shooting stars. "Make a vow," said the skin. "It is customary to make a vow when you see a shooting star." I seized the opportunity. I made a vow to pay my ancient debt, to recompense my fellow travellers along the way for everything which I had taken illegally.

Of all the memories which haunted me, there was one which was more persistent than the others—I was one of those old-time actresses, always prepared to shed blood or tears. One of those actresses who, each time, built her existence beat by beat, scene by scene, act by act, without suspecting for a single instant that she was not inventing her life each time but only recapitulating it. She also enjoyed, like so many other evolved types, wallowing in self-satisfaction, priding herself on being someone exceptional. In short, seeing herself, though bang in the middle of the herd, as a superior being.

With no regard for anyone else, the old actress built her unbreachable fortress stone by stone, out of empty dreams and misdirections. It was a sight to see her defending her castle in Spain, invoking all her authority and power for her egotistical, personal ambitions. When the day came that the drama of her existence entered its pathetic phase, that is, when there was nothing left for this dear old crazy lady to do but die at the end of the play, when she could not, in future, add one more brocade curtain to the illusory beauty of her terrestrial scenery, the ancient ancestress died weeping in despair, with not a soul to hear her.

For several hours, in this testing dream, some voices like the wind asked me to take up my pain, to bear my sufferings because they were the fruits of my own actions. But what can one do to remain lucid and loving in this time of cataclysm and desertion? Indeed, what can one do to remain aware of one's deeds faced with unfathomable disappointment? Or with fates that confound the clearest of spirits? Not to speak of proofs of famines and wars which seem to hurl themselves at us like destitution on the poor?

Can one be conscious, fully conscious, without ever looking back? Without turning, trembling, toward the sidereal wake of our past anterior on the Wheel of Rebirth? Without imagining that our existences gravitate about a central pivot and that we are sailing along the river of the transmigration of souls? That between all the living and all the dead there lies but a single superb layer—a layer of magnetic roots which bear us toward the theatre of memory, the promised land of our metamorphoses, where, while recapitulating the past, we learn and understand. In this land where clarity penetrates our hearts, we instantly recognize those whom we call our friends, our lovers, when we enfold their cherished presences in our arms.

And what about the other ones? All those others with whom we have exchanged blows, silent blows which have raked our hearts and sometimes made our blood gleam? We fight against them, all those others, standing upon the memories of a thousand years. Let us take revenge! Let us close our eyes to their good qualities. We cry out against injustice, we howl that they are our enemies without being aware that we call them so out of long-standing habit.

But, in the end, it doesn't matter much whether or not you believe in the transmigration of souls on the Wheel of Rebirth. For it appears that all people progress in the period of their own rule according to the rhythm of fever and form, following their impulses to cross boundaries, and submitting to disintegrations which defy matter. They pursue inspirations and aspirations, never ceasing to modulate the music of ashes and resurrection. One must not hurry slow things.

In those times which shortly preceded the foundation of the red cicadas, there was, among the lesbians as everywhere else on earth, a strong demand for illumination. This need for light was as stimulating and irresistible as an electrical storm over Niagara Falls. Something wanted to appear! Something wanted to appear and this thing would appear gradually, ready to introduce something new into our minds. We would finally enter a more humane age, an age which would direct every ray of our energies toward the knowledge and recognition of other people. An age in which we would make the effort to become more sensitive, more receptive to the messages reaching us from other solar systems, when we would make a superhuman effort to capture the voices of the stars, of others, of the future. It was phenomenal!

We were so stimulated that our cranial cases vibrated and the minds of women and men both were illuminated. Old structures collapsed— whatever had lasted too long to last another second crumbling, crumbling into dust. This produced enormous, absolutely illegal and quite delightful explosions all over the earth, nowhere more noisily than in the West. Everyone asked everyone else about electromagnetic, seismic, Hertzian waves. We were aboard a train of telepathic, telephonic, telegraphic, and explosive waves. Yes, indeed, everyone was asking everyone else and all the Churches and Holy Chapels had to respond to the lively rumours which they could not, from then on, bury under a couple of shovelfuls of infallibility.

For the first time in history, we lesbians did not want to withdraw in fear and shame from the aversion we knew we usually provoked. No more question of internalizing suspicions and accusations or of feeling guilty for whatever they might imagine about us. Especially among certain men . . . men to whom gaining access to Gomorrah, they thought, would be like getting to know one of the prehistoric jungles which still haunts the human memory—mammalian reptiles, bitches with tiger's teeth, pernicious, carnivorous, evil flowers, an amphibious octopus stretching its arms around the Tree of Good and Evil. Not daring to risk sounding such dizzying depths, they stayed where they were, on the edge of the Gomorrah Canyon, with a panic of passengers.

Spurred on by this highly evolved period, we came out into the open in our thousands and thousands. The old simplicity of invisibility could no longer keep us in line. No more hiding us in the closet to live like moles. We marched through the streets of the most important cities of North America in close-packed ranks, flanked by a minuscule part of the feminist movement and by our political allies, the male homosexuals. We established magazines, presses, lesbian archives. Historians studied our genesis. Well-known women writers came out in their stories and autobiographical novels with insane pride. And with a great deal of courage, dignity, and sincerity. The concerted effect of all these energies made us still more determined to take our place in the sun, to confront the world, and to launch ourselves into infinity in the exaltation of freedom. It made us determined to seek out and find those places where this earthly mutation could survive with a minimum of external constraint, those places where we could at last overstep our own internal limits and develop a lightning-clear vision of our future. Each of us wished that all over the world, the powers-that-be would finally develop their amorous, intellectual, and material capacities. That was why in those eventful days lesbians established little communities on the east and west coasts of North America.

The Appalachian one was started by my dear Montreal lesbian old guard. They talked about the "luxury of our retreat." Actually, the old guard was composed largely of retired women—librarians, nurses, teachers, a real estate agent. I call them my "dear old guard" because I have felt great tenderness for them for a long time. In the old days, when I came across these women in the streets or bars or cafes, my heart would start to beat faster—I could see in them stray sparks which could spread in a flash and suddenly make themselves known like a forest fire. Most often, it was at that time when night reveals its pits of loneliness that I would see them strolling, walking slowly, their hair short and greying or already white, their clothing also grey. They looked uneasy and were looking for other women whom they knew were profoundly out of step with everyone else's life and schedule. Too far ahead or too far behind.

Sometimes they put me in mind of lemurs, those little primates which are first in order of importance in the mysterious history of evolution. These shy lemurs come out primarily at night. In the piercing silence, they move across the earth and into the trees, just like the wandering spirits of ancient civilizations. But is it truly timidity that makes them act this way? Could it be a keen sense of mortality?

When I came to this area, the old guard had been living there for almost a decade. They had beautiful wood or stone houses whose slate roofs were in harmony with the nature of this half-wild plateau, half-hidden by the bewitching forest where one could let oneself wander in order to fall under a spell. A mountainous escarpment, seven times as old as the Rocky Mountains, encircled the plateau. Toward the east, a beaver pond and a turbulent river. In the summer, if you were paddling on the river and if you happened to be wearing your friendliest expression on that particular day, a whisky jack would alight on the bow of your canoe where he would look you over from all sides, right down to your oldest soul, while keeping in constant motion in his dance of curiosity. At the extreme point of this plateau, a sheet of ice swollen with rocks at one time descended from Hudson's Bay in monstrous chaos, carved out a deep valley, and left behind a lake filled with dark water and crisscrossed by loons.

It is, in fact, an odd area. As odd as the loons which have haunted the lakes since the Miocene—sixty million years is the measure which light and imagination take their time to cross. The loons lived on earth before us and even before most other birds. In the country, everyone recognizes the loon, that slightly mad bird which speaks to the moon. Ornithologists have not yet reached agreement about the repertoire of the loon's various calls. One group says it has four calls, another claims five. There's that brief, warbling note heard just before he shoots his body like a torpedo toward the bottom of the lake to catch a fish. And that other call, the long, long note, held till it pierces your heart. Unquestionably, there is no other nocturnal cry sadder or more penetrating anywhere on this earth. Nor should we forget his laugh—when he brings his voice from his chest to his head in a joyful yodel. Or when he responds to the nostalgic song of the coyotes by baying like a dog. And finally, that joy-filled cry made by a mated pair which has found each other after a long separation.

There, you see—five calls, not four! But the Native Americans say there are really six. We've overlooked the voice of divine truth, that call which the loon makes just before storms, definitely announcing chaotic somersaults of snow-filled clouds and blizzard winds along the dorsal spine of the mountains which reveal an ancient, terrifying geological scene—their rugged south faces, their smooth and polished north slopes, as if under sneak attack from the rear.

Before that geologic drama, the mountains of the Appalachians and of all of New England, their heads swept by the sky, were as tall as the Himalayas are today. But one day, a force unknown, clashing and spurting with trap doors and cyclones of ice, cut off their heads to a depth of nine kilometres of rock. This glacial sheet, breaking over them like one stride of a colossal sheep with voracious teeth and sharp hooves, left to the mountains only their roots. And add to that, past the beaver pond where the undergrowth of moss and ferns begins, the ghostly site of a village—smashed walls, gaping cellars half-filled with dirt and deposits of greenish sand. The dead tree roots which wrap about these remains are a perfect likeness of a boa constrictor's embrace.

It is a cursed region, the old guard related. A foul and mysterious crime toward the end of the Seventeenth Century—since that day, evidently, the village has been stalked by death. They talk about suicides, an axe murder, arson, of gullied earth borne to the bottom of the valley. They talk about entire families going mad and about wolves, mountain lions, coyotes, Indians, and a "savage and howling nature," as a minister from Boston, straying into our area, put it more than a century ago.

"But you've settled here despite all this."

"When we moved in, we wouldn't wander too far afield," the old guard answered.

"What were you afraid of?"

"Of becoming bewitched ourselves!"

"By whom? By what?"

"By nature, in the first place."

"And after nature?"

"By self-hatred."

"But self-hatred seems more like an obstacle than an enchantment," I said.

"No! It is a spell."

They all said the same thing, without any embellishment. The look that one of them gave me had the sudden and exact acuteness of a clairvoyant. The logic of this group disappeared.

"In the mountains, spells come together by themselves, like clouds or trees of the same species."

"If I understand you correctly," I said, "there was some kind of bad energy in the air here?"

There was a pause, a kind of wavering. My question seemed to have brought them back too abruptly to a period of dangers and misfortunes.

"The evil energy was not in the air. On the contrary. It was waiting for us, rooted in a lizard dozing in the sun."

"Is it really that powerful?" I asked, intrigued.

"Stronger than the united force of all our personalities," they answered in lowered voices.

"But what is its source?"

"The primary form of this evil kind of energy arises from nature itself—from the harshness of the climate, the dark forest which resembles the threshold of a black door, the blasts of wind off the rocky peaks, the glacial isolation, the nocturnal noises. All of these things absorb you, take hold of you within, and revive vast prophecies of death in your memory."

"And the second form?"

"That comes from the weather."

"But wait a minute," I exclaimed in pain, "the weather is a blessing. The changing weather is a natural harvest rich in exquisite flavours . . ."

"Not if the weather turns you inside out like a glove. Not if the weather strips off your years the way a snake sloughs its skin."

"What happened?"

There was a profound silence. The old guard averted their eyes. Sometimes in a conversation a question that is too direct closes more doors than it opens. We can force open doors without respecting the treasures and secrets those doors protect. Whether these doors open once again is mysterious, since we are guardians of graves. Through a slippery process which was going on in both my mind and my heart, I tried to find the right words to defuse the silence.

"I came to live at the start of the Appalachian trail, as did you, to think, to build, and to revitalize my life. And yet . . ."

"And yet?"

"I have to sleep all the time. Emotionally, I find myself plunged into general sleepiness."

"And intellectually?"

"Completely dazed—comatose!"

"That was the spell taking its toll," said one red cicada, shivering.

"Something is creeping into you and finding no opposition," another one added. "Before you even know what's hit you, you regress into the lowest regions of your mind. You no longer react to anything which is part of the culture of your own time. Nothing can distract you any more—suspended in isolation and the inborn fear of death, you launch yourself in pursuit of times past and into frantic physical activity in which you can absorb yourself completely. In subtle gradations, you desert the realm of human thought. You throw yourself into physical activity—from dawn to dusk you plough, you dig, you weed, you carry, you pick, and you eat. Day after day, with your mind completely empty, you do what you did the day before, caught in all the magnetic fluids of the trees, the rocks and the animals.

"And by night? By night the mind dreams with such frightful openness that it is marked by a wing which can hold its place on a branch above a sea of waving leaves, ready to join the blue layer which flows beneath and which is neither sky nor starry space but a torrent-filled river running toward the gulfs."

"But how can you reverse this appeal? How can you resist this energy which carries you away?"

"Well," they answered, dodging the question, "what have you done?"

"I wrote a lecture for myself."

"But you're a novelist! Why didn't you gather the materials for a novel or a story?"

"So I could avoid the triple curse of the novelist, according to the sainted Katherine Ann Porter—self-examination, self-preoccupation, and self-pity. In the novel, as in every creative form, it is difficult to construct its words from something of value, from something which has the most direct connection to the heart of every living being. If, through a failure of insight, our creative works are not vital, useful, and helpful, they almost always appear destructive. This time, I wanted to get in tune with other people in an 'other' kind of way."

"What was your lecture about?"

"Women's literary adventure. I'm using the word *literary* in the same sense that it was used in the 17th century when they talked about 'people of fine minds and pleasing literature'. The human adventure is as much spiritual as it is cultural, political, and scientific. I've been collecting unpublished information for a long time about images of learned women and pioneers from every continent, women galactic explorers who bring together solar ruptures, fogs of Martian red matter, the desire spilt by the liquid prairies of Venus and human pain and the mortal violence of our passions. Drawing on the work of these women, I had the sense of drawing on the stuff of universal thought, even if History is silent on the matter."

"And after that?"

"After that, I was burning with the desire to transmit this substance which dealt with life and creation to other generations just as a family secret or an alchemical formula is transmitted. So, going on the road, I visited all the little villages of the Appalachians, going where I might encounter this adventure—that is, in those places where women, men, and children gather round the fire, food, and books. I spoke in kitchens, living rooms, parish halls and church basements."

"What was the reaction?"

"The idea that such remarkable women had existed and that even today we could come close to them as they had come close to us, by means of a lecture, created a tremor of enthusiasm and admiration."

"That's how I avoided falling under the spell," I added after a moment. "But how did you elude it?"

"Through astrology!"

They said this word in one encompassing voice, showing that they had a deep respect for it. The veil they had just drawn back permitted another to be seen which was just as mysterious.

Oh, if only one could skip over dreary days the way one skips pages in a book to quickly recover those passages where the shiver of a double life and the magic substance of encounters with omens appears like a watermark.

"You consulted an astrologer? Did you want to know the personal fate of each of you?" I asked.

"If astrology is a prophetic art, then the role of the prophet is a risky one."

"Then you believe that destiny is in one's own hands?"

"You cannot confuse fate and destiny."

"To distinguish illusion from reality?"

"Human intelligence will be able to do that more and more. The great astrological wheel does not impose its will—on the contrary, it indicates that the influences are evenly distributed and that we are all equal on the astral road."

"If you didn't want to learn each individual's fate, then why did you consult an astrologer?"

"To find out what signs of the Zodiac govern our community! Each human gathering has its own virtues and particular qualities as well as its gross personal illnesses and its poisoning of the spirit."

"Are countries also subject to the influence of the stars? I never thought of that before," I added, enthralled.

"Just like human beings, they are both pervaded by the stars which influence their personalities and illuminated by sidereal conjunctions which permeate their spirits."

"Think about Canada, for example, or the United States, or even France!"

"Canada, for example, is under the signs of Libra and Taurus, while the United States, obviously, is under the signs of Gemini and Aquarius. As for France . . ."

"Let me guess! Since France once lit up the world with its revolution, I presume that it is a Leo."

"And its rising sign is Pisces."

"I suppose the same thing applies to cities and towns?"

"Well, yes, to a certain extent. But the influence is less marked."

"The stars and personality, the stars and the spirit?"

"That is all relative to the degree to which you've evolved. What is your sign?"

"I'm Aquarius with Leo rising. I'm prey to periodic imbalances."

"Like Russia," said an ironic voice.

"But how fascinating it all is—Russia and the United States both Aquarius."

"There are no other countries under that sign. But, pay attention—Aquarius is the sign of your spirit."

"My ascendent?"

"Yes. It can also be called the sign of completion, of consummation. At the present moment, it appears that the United States and Russia are governed by their personality signs—Gemini for the U.S. and Leo for the Soviet Union."

"And how can it happen in one's essential personality to be a separatist and self-centred?"

"The personality sign is like a rain cloud which shrouds the light for a moment. Outside, everything is glowing in the serene sphere of the external face."

"Of course! But what if the personality tries to escape from ignorance?"

"If the personality would move out of egocentricity into altruism, it will certainly have to unite itself with the conjunction of the stars which governs its spirit."

"What happens then?"

"It will symbolically die and be reborn in the light and the air. It will finally be free!"

With a gentle rustling, like the wings of a bird coming to light, I felt a tide of tenderness for the old guard making its way through my veins. There it is, I thought, ever and always, that connection which binds all things together, kindling new conditions and changes which sometimes look like miracles."

"Now I am beginning to understand why you wanted a full-scale horoscope for the foundation of your community."

"In the days when the spell was launching one of its sneak attacks on what we were undertaking, we knew that we would have to work to understand those ancient influences under which humanity has lived for so long."

"You were waiting on the stars?"

"Yes, for enlightenment. For the shedding of light."

Shining like the Amazon's double-bladed axe, the words went by, cleaving the air without a sound.

"There was a time once when what we call a birth certificate was a horoscope," one of them reminded us, her eyes closed in order to stay for a long time in the interior of memory. "When a child was born, the parents were taught about its resistance, its inclinations, its weaknesses and its strong points. They were taught about planetary activity and about everything that could stifle or nourish this new life."

"But all this has only a remote connection with our culture. No matter who would be astonished by it," I said, looking disconcerted. "The chart of your planetary influences was certainly revealing at that point."

"Revealing and disconcerting," they answered after a slight hesitation.

"And then what? And then what?"

I was insisting, charged up with the idea of exploring the secret of the stars to the very end and inserting it into the framework of my existence.

"The community began to exist on earth, legitimately, in the summer, in the glare of the heat of both day and night, at a time almost exactly between the summer solstice and the autumnal equinox."

"That's the season of night-time fairies, of the Perseid showers. I like to pretend that the trajectory of the shooting stars brushes the forehead of the Great Bear. All right! The community is Leo, then."

"Daughters of fire! Each of us darting into the motion of the flames of the next one in the process of becoming."

"All those who recognize themselves as the dramatic centre of their universe say the same thing. I can detect a fundamentally dangerous rage in your triumphant tones," I added warily.

"You are probably right—the most superficial aspect of personality can stifle the beatings of the heart. When the astrologer revealed our ascendent sign to us, she brought us back to the radiant surface of the earth," one voice went on, as weary as if night were falling.

"I don't want to make a mistake—Taurus—plunging forward, desire, sense of duty, and delight in the concrete."

"No, Virgo—the guts of time, immobility."

"Virgos are always discontented," I said lightly.

"Immobility," they repeated, "while life is a moving path, a road to travel."

"I don't really understand your disappointment. We're told that Virgo is the oldest of the signs and that the matriarchy was founded under her."

"They also say that by mating with Leo, she gave rise to the Sphinx. The depths, darkness, peace and quiet, everything we firmly rejected," they added in an aggrieved tone.

"It sounds as though you're only thinking about power and about the superiority that planetary influences might grant you over the rest of humanity."

"You're not being fair. We were thinking about evolving. But the astrologer said that we'd missed the boat."

"I thought prophesying was a risky business."

"She was only expressing her predictions."

"What did she deduce?"

"That the Virgin had chained the Lion and sacrificed him."

"And what does that mean in actual fact?"

"Disenchantment, disillusion, internal strife, and disagreements."

"But surely there is some way to counteract that."

"Only by abandoning our collective plan and starting on a new cycle. We were considering dissolving the community."

"Then what happened?"

"I was stretched out in bed, exhausted," said one. "The feeling we were all experiencing had not yet been identified, but I was entirely under its influence."

"Saying 'defeat' too often was aging us," another said.

"I remember, it was almost dark . . ." said someone else.

"The rain was lightly tapping on the roofs of our houses when she arrived with the first animal," another said.

"Who? Who?" I asked, already halfway up this height that curiosity or a tragic sense of life had brought us.

"Noria," a troubled voice answered.

Third Song
The Lion of Bangor

Dawn! At last the running rivers of light make their appearance. Overnight, a snow storm has powdered the trees with winter. This morning, the forests are bending under the weight of the *qali*. The *qali*? In this part of the world, this is a little fragment of our descent into hell, and no doubt about it. But for the arctic animals, it is an embodiment of survival and for the forests, it is an architect, a logger, a shaper. *Qali* attaches itself to the branches and bends or breaks them, so that a hole in the tree cover is opened which, from spring through till autumn, will let in all the light the young shoots need to grow, drawing them toward the sky. On these young shoots, the hoofed mammals browse throughout the ferocious winter.

I hear the music of a plane's engine. The lowered lights of the engine, the white mountains, the cold which hangs clouds from so many notches in the sky—how lovely it all is. On the Appalachian plateau, the *qali* is settled in; it has a hard and granitelike sparkle. The little plane slowly comes down, like an unanticipated angel. Is this our reward? Will we deserve this fleeting grace in our graves? Is it finally, my dears, the moment of our resurrection? The moment when all the souls of the children of earth will mingle in person; that is, is it the moment of the dramatic art of the creation of the world? Of the action and labour of those inexplicable attenuating circumstances which unite us, one with the other, across birth and death?

"And well beyond that," the Angel of the Here breathed to me.

"Is it absolutely indispensable to enter into this cosmic drama? One wave of the hand, and there you have a radiant, astronomical, geological, botanical representation in the dawn's blaze, the torrential mountain streams, the plants of immortality. And the clouds sail on and humans are born, full of comedy and tragedy. Is it absolutely indispensable?"

"Exhausting but indispensable. And anyway, how else would you have it? How else would you have things on Earth?"

"Is it a sacred duty?"
"You must do it. You must fulfill the duty."
I know, I know . . . For one another."
"For the Angel of the Night."
"Who is that?"
"Earth."
"Earth of the times never to be forgotten?"
"Earth while waiting for your final transfiguration."
"I have never seen this Angel."
"That's because you're always asleep."
"When can he be seen?"
"The Angel of the Night shows himself between midnight and the moment when the stars in the constellation of the Great Bear become invisible."
"Since I was a child I've got up at dawn to do my accounts and reconstruct my debts."
"Good for you. But is it enough?"
"There is also a way through the splendid dawn where you can surrender, if you want to."
"So there is. Surrender and . . . ?"
"And anticipate."
"Anticipate a presence?"
"Yes. The presence of eternity."
"What are you going to do now?"
"Write."

I have some white sheets under my hand, a light wad, lowing like a cloud. The sheets are perishable and provisional as we all are; but they are equally familiar with our griefs, our doubts, our sorrows, and our fears. In friendship and in love they are the witnesses of all those who read and those who write. It is our duty to look at them, to engrave them so deeply and passionately inside ourselves that they will be resurrected one day along with the rest of us, beyond the reach of pain.

Like something brought back from a distant journey—out there, in my own domain, I was a fabulous beast with wings to my ankles—it is a time in my life when I should live by myself. I feel myself tremble because I know how difficult that will be. Whatever it is in us that demands solitude also demands we be with others.

I have my white sheets at hand and I want to write on them with passion and pride about me and for you. It is so much easier to write out of oneself in opposition to them, to bury oneself, an old burrowing beast, for cycle after cycle in subterranean layers of melancholy and absurdity. Or even, through the combination of provocation and talent, to inflict one's gall, one's verdigrised carapace, one's poisoned sucker. Come on! Throw up! Blow your nose and mop your brow and take aim. Aim carefully. All the better if there's a heart in your line of fire. And if your terrorist acts wind up sounding stale, then wave the sword of Damocles, that spear of moonless nights which kindles this awkward mirage, this mysterious object which we call the personality.

To write about the conquest of space when the human soul, not wanting to be separated from heaven, stands erect, drawn by the immense creative force of memory, contrary to the forgetfulness which holds sway among the children of the earth.

I am thinking about that rooster, duck, and sheep that were launched in a balloon against the high grey drapery of the clouds in the fall of 1783. I am upset by the image of a dog. She died in November, 1958 in space, after seven days in orbit when the batteries controlling the air in her doghouse ran out. In a Fotokronika colour photo from Tass, Laïka looks at us. She knows she is going to die— the iris in her crystalline eyeball drops like the hammer on a revolver and a thousand tears, welling from the depths of the tear ducts, that house where her mother and father were born, roll toward us, opening up a passage through space.

Airplanes! Old crates, chicken coops, the new space cavalry mounts its winged horses stripped to essentials. The real cavalry of all the world armies disappeared when the first biplanes flew over the front in 1914 during the First World War. What seemed, at the beginning, to be an extraordinary adventure marked by the spirit of romance— respect for the enemy's courage, pity if he proved too weak or in trouble—was transformed, with demented speed, into a gigantic enterprise of death.

Why? Why do the same things always happen? Milarepa, the madman of Tibet, said that the inevitability of impermanence attaches itself to everything the sun shines on—that sooner or later, for one reason or another, even innocence must confront decay.

Airplanes! In those days, it must have required a transcendent talent or a mysterious power to launch yourself toward the stars in one of those unstable machines, whose steering was inadequate and whose engine often stalled in mid-air. You flew surrounded by the smell of castor oil, gasoline, canvas, and freshly varnished wood. The propellers sang in their marvellous language. The song mounted toward the subtly essenced sky, aerial exchanges with the principalities of angels, tumult, scent of adventure, the sun's playing over the soul of the wings, over the fuselage, over the roundness of the engine housing, ecstasies, rapid dive, tailspin and, from so far above to so far below, what piercing star guided your course in the night-time wind? What is the name of your lucky star?

The star that keeps watch over Noria, which kept her from fading away, and which dominated her magnetically was called Sirius. Sirius shines in the throat of the silvery constellation Canis Major, the Great Dog, whose voice is like the chiming of a bell in the northern wind. Sirius is also called the star of sensitivity—it initiates all of us on earth to every form of life. When night falls and the darkness begins to spill its basket of stars, they say the daytime birds sing once again for Sirius.

As for myself, Jeanne, the Polar Star, the one you see with your head tilted back crossing the seas, keeps an eye on me. It lives in the constellation of Ursa Minor, the Little Bear. This is the star of reorientation—it helps us find what we have wasted and lost. Under the fiery eye of the comets, it can also carry us with cyclonic speed to the original source of the emotions of the multitude.

Noria has just landed on the plateau in her Spad.

For the aviatrixes and aviators of the '20s, the biplane was the best kind of airplane. Brought into the world by Deperdussin—it was the first plane to break the two hundred kph mark in full flight—Spad first stood for *Société Provisoire des Aéroplanes Deperdussin* until the business went bankrupt, then the *Société Pour L'Aviation et ses Dérivés*. Noria's paternal grandfather, who was mixed up in this bankruptcy, used to say that the name Spad stemmed from several languages like Esperanto and Volapuk. Noria says that this was absolutely untrue.

Equipped with the famous Hispano-Suiza engine, the Spad could attain an engine speed of 215 kph. At cruising speed, it could remain aloft for close to six hours; at top speed, for more than two. From head to tail, with its flexed canvas, its stabilizer with its triangular aileron, all it carried into the sky was streamlined. Even the propeller blades, painted like saw teeth, pushed it toward the sky where it was metamorphosed into a bird of prey in colour, in music, going at the same pace as the clouds and the wind.

"In a moment of exhaustion or exaltation, who has not dreamt of one day being an object?" Noria said, coming back in with the dogs.

"A piano, a violin, a cello . . ."

"Or an animal. To escape the horror of one's self."

I'm not so young any more, I thought, looking at her. I can't wait until someone desires me. I'm not the woman still young and full of promise who left Montreal. They say that women possess that ideal feeling and that ideal comprehension essential to the transmission of the art of loving and living together. But love exhausts the blood and erodes the time and strength of women, too. One passes from deep affection to the warpath in a single leap, hypnotized by one's own choice.

"Child, I've often dreamt that I was a bird," Noria said. "I told myself today that the Spad is the carcass of an old American bird . . ."

"Or one of those white cranes that soar above the deltas, examining everything with its yellow eyes . . ."

"A condor?"

"Why not a masked ibis standing guard over the unknown grave of an aviatrix?"

"The Spad is a red vulture that cleanses bodies and souls," Noria thrust in. "The sparks from the engine light up the bird's guts, liver, and nerves. And I feel myself enveloped by a wave, bound by the etherial substance of the aerial bodies gravitating around the mountains."

"Tell me the story again," I said. "You know . . ."

"I know, I know," Noria said, her face lighting up.

This story gives me such pleasure, I thought, because it provides me with an unparalleled sense of security. I love to hear it over and over and I am more attached to it than to any other story in the world.

"On this particular day, I was flying above the Appalachian Trail. I had taken off from Bangor even though the weather was rather bad and I was headed toward the northern tip of Maine when all

55

of a sudden, clouds of snow blew up in a sky made of black net.

"Even after all this time, it still seems to me that I was mired in these clouds in a single second, at three thousand meters, stopped in a way that defied all resistance, all flight. The needle on the thermometer began to rise and rise . . . The water would not circulate and started to boil with an evil smell of resentment. The fatal moment was approaching when all of this life fluid would evaporate and the engine would stop, burnt out by what it could not stand.

"The thermometer needle was close to one hundred degrees and I could only point the plane's nose up and try to fly above the clouds, preferably without causing the engine to overheat. All the lights on the instrument panel were red when the Spad began to lose altitude. The battle it wanted to wage against this leaden mass was lost in advance. Terrified, I switched on the radio, even though I probably wouldn't be able to hear anything because of the storm and the howling of the winds. Wireless voices, radio-navigator voices, mortal voices—where were you then?

"The only thing left to do was to shove the stick forward and cut the gas. It was intensely hot as I did this and I could hardly budge the throttle because it was burning hot. I was hoping to fall and to take advantage of the weight of the fall to burst through the clouds and restart the machine close to the ground, just before it would be all over.

"I fell. It was like being mounted on nausea. When falling, you lose your hands and feet first. Then your leaden chest and your stomach full of needles. And when you are submerged in the anguish of no longer being, you lose your mind and your soul.

"No, your life does not pass in front of your eyes. Neither do your various conditions of soul. That's all silly. That's all vain. You don't think about your mother or your father or your lovers. There is no one there—they're all gone. Absence, death, and whatever comes after death enter your mind like a cold metal bar. It is an unforgettable moment of affection for yourself.

"I fell. I had an appointment. With whom? What? A miracle, a rescue? An angel which would show itself to me in all the beauty of its gentle wings of paradisal light? No—I had an appointment with something in which I had never wanted to believe at all— with pity. From life to life, pity, mercy. Something which comes down from above to this place, to us.

"Half-senseless, I fell. Suddenly, three hundred metres below the little plane, the Maine forests appeared. I had fallen more than twenty-seven hundred metres. The thermometer was now at eighty degrees and the pressure gauge at zero. The engine had stopped during the drop. I made the plane glide just above the birches, the ash trees, and the flaming sugar maples. I banked and turned on the gas with the auxiliary throttle which regulates carburation at various altitudes. The engine restarted.

"I felt that my life had shifted, that my centre of gravity now lay in the propeller blades and that I was straining with all my strength toward these steel blades which spun through the air.

"I pointed the Spad up to gain some altitude. I entered a boiling mist which gradually recovered Mount Katahdin with its sharpened peaks overlooking this region of lakes, chasms, and canyons cut deeply into the slate. In spring, this is the first mountain in all of North America the rising sun shines on. They whisper that a terrible deity, the Pamola, lives here, a relic of the Toltec zodiac, a prophetic bird which signifies the fulfillment of destiny. If you should trudge, wounded, through this region, it will come to peck at your still-living flesh; if you do not vibrate to the same chords as the Lord of the Night, you will be stricken with delirium and wake up to find yourself disintegrated.

"I was afraid of coming upon a mountain. Go up, go up and shatter myself in mid-flight on that scree. Descend and ignite with the autumnal forests. Go straight on toward those unbreachable walls and put an end to the whole undertaking. I had neither the time nor the room to make a turn without catching the wings. And to think that I had begun this trip with such joy.

"All of a sudden, the radio, which I had forgotten, began to whistle like a blackbird and then to roar like a flood of water, a huge fire. A demented vibrational activity—reception was impossible, the message inaudible. But someone was calibrating the radio in a different way. Someone was violently improving the receiver. In the ether, someone was freely reversing the golden thread of the waves, the fluids, and the telepathic fields. Someone was amplifying the sound waves and enlarging our ear drums. Who? One of those whose name is too terrible to be said out loud? A guardian of the threshold. An accompanist.

"I was submerged. My little transaction with death was altogether disrupted. The radio was communicating a succession of impressions and impulses and I didn't have time to erect a shell to protect myself from them. A fiery arrow shot through my head when I heard the voice of my mother, dead so long ago, so long ago.

" 'Straight ahead,' she shouted. ' "Straight ahead! Head for the peaks!'

"She spoke so violently and with such force that every energy-filled word was propelled and struck me.

" 'Straight ahead!' she shouted once again.

"The mountain walls were approaching with their sharp ridges. Impassable. Suddenly, to the left, between the peaks, a corridor the colour of a blue skate . . .

" 'No,' my mother screamed, 'go straight ahead!'

" 'But there's a way through,' I shouted back.

" 'No! That's a dead end.'

" 'But I can't go back!'

" 'Go toward the peaks! Toward the peaks!' my mother's strong voice shouted once again.

"Everything on the instrument panel was swelling. Ahead of the engine housing and at the wing tips, a vacuum was pulling. The slate-grey walls of the mountain were only an arm's length away.

" 'Mother, I can't go back there!'

" 'There's a breach—you can get through.'

"There, right in front of me, the mountain was split in two. The rudder obeyed me. I hardly had to nose the plane up. The gap seemed to open up like a compass card. I committed myself to this passage. I climbed and the knotted wires stood out, showers of sparks. Chunks of stone fell as the plane flew by. Then my wake became snowy. I was flying over the descending slopes on the other side of Mount Katahdin.

"The radio was now silent.

"I glided.

"Ahead of me, the whole visual field of the Appalachians picked out in blue the falls, the cascades, the lakes, the points of light, the rivers, and the crystal which the sky grasps from everywhere with the blue of its devotion. And then there were the most beautiful forests of all of America.

"To the north, I could see crosswinds fraying an ocean of clouds which were approaching. I was almost out of fuel. I had to change direction."

"You flew to us," I said.

"I didn't know that then. I was looking for a landing field."

"And a refuge for your precious cargo."

"For my passengers," Noria corrected me.

"And you went back there?"

"Yes. I flew over the mountain peaks."

"And?"

"I saw the corridor I wanted to take and the split rock wall further away. The corridor led to a giant wall made of angular blocks. I could never have got through. The breach was the only passage. Do you think I'm crazy?"

"Each time I hear this story, I think you're a little less crazy. Even despite that glint of light."

"What glint?"

"The one shut up in the pupil of your eye and which sometimes gets loose and starts to vibrate—like now."

"It's a little piece of the North Star," Noria said, and smiled.

"Everything you've told me is absolutely true, I know."

"I checked it out with the weather office—the storm I escaped from was almost as bad at times as the one which pounded New England in 1934. On the mountain tops, the wind got up to two hundred kph. The New Atlantis coastal storms always form in the Arctic. We live in the most dangerous climactic zone on the continent."

"A forgotten fragment of the Himalayas! Where were you in 1934?"

"Where were you?"

"I was going to land on earth," I say.

"In 1934, I was three years old and I was living in a hole with my mother. A hellhole. Wooden walls under waving canvas roofs. Hangars filled with towropes, suitcases, human shouts, and the thunder of those steel birds who sang when you wanted them to spit out their dirty oil. Straw mattresses thrown on the floor and paper-thin blankets. I grew up under the propellers.

"In my memory I carry a topographic map of the hell where I stayed with my mother. It was an existence of exhaustion and despair, from airfield to airfield with my mother constantly repeating, 'They don't believe in women in this country.'"

"She was a courageous woman."

"She was a born leader—she drew her strength from the great reservoir of universal life through the power of her implacable will. She was a mother to be proud of. She would never betray because her loyalty was founded on an absolute absence of fear. But she was also hard, obstinate, and so awfully arrogant!"

"The arrogance of the tyrant?"

"The arrogance of the self-taught. She seemed torn apart by an interior struggle as if everything had to be born in pain and unending grief. When she comforted me when I was unhappy, she became very distant, closed in upon herself."

"You take after her . . ."

"She was active and had a physical and moral courage which was equal to anything. I am lazy and often put things off," Noria said.

"But you are always prepared to adopt a desperate cause or defend the weak."

"The older I get, the more extravagant I become, since what really matters at the end of this century is intellectual liveliness. 'Intelligence!' my mother used to say. 'Everywhere we look there is a new form of intelligence and will. That is the essential difference between the 20th Century and every other century. A radiant balance has developed gradually among affection, love, devotion, intelligence, and will.'

"She would gently lay her hands on an airplane wing and add, 'This is only the beginning, Noria. Young as you are, you will see prodigies and miracles. You are finally going to make up for all the time we wasted in our stagecoaches, our boats, our streetcars and our buses.'"

"How old was she then?"

"She was thirty. And she looked twenty years older. The physical torments she had undergone beating endurance, speed and distance records had aged her. 'Up there,' she used to tell me, 'the air is fire; it sets fire to your skin until your heart, tortured by the altitude, sounds the alarm and your brain denies you like something unimportant.'

"And then there were those crazy acrobatic stunts where she risked her life but the crowd loved so much."

"What did she do?"

"Oh, for example, she used to land on a roof between two electric lines. Or take off from the narrow corridor of Broadway in New York City. Or fly between two rows of trees along a narrow, winding road. Or glide over the water for five minutes or more with her engine off.

"Just flying was never enough! They demanded more and more dangerous stunts and the pilots had to push their machines to the limits of their resistance in order to please the public.

"The first plane she flew was the lightest and fastest in the world. At least that's what the builder advertised."

"Was he lying?"

"He forgot to say that it was a dangerous and unstable engine which would land at almost eighty kph without shocks and with inadequate brakes. My mother would brake the plane by grabbing the tires with her gloved hands.

"Oh, I know what you're thinking," Noria murmured in a voice as full of patience as if she were tending to a child's fragility.

Who thought what? I thought. I am a hundred-thousand-year-old lady who takes the time to listen to marvellous tales, in hope of eradicating the meanness in her spirit.

"Your mother must have been a marvellous woman," I said. "Difficult, egotistical, childish. But absolutely unique and captivating. She wanted to achieve her ideal—to become an airplane or to be crushed by the plane and the crowd which wanted her in the plane."

"That's right. Like so many others who would die crashing down on out-of-the-way airfields," Noria added, her mind turning back to the past. "Like the rest of them, she wanted to fly and to own her own plane. In those days, planes were sold the way luxury cars are today. It set you apart . . ."

"You were one of the best. But your mother said that they didn't believe in women in this country."

"In women pilots! But of course they could be workers. They put together the fabric of the canvas, checking to see it was solid and properly taut and tightened the airfoils. Or they could be mechanics and tune the engines, mount the propellers, install and maintain the weapons, which consisted of a Vickers machine gun timed so that it fired its whistling bullets across the propeller, and two light machine guns which the mechanics coupled to fire defensively. Naturally, they did all this work for lower wages than men."

"Were there a lot of them in the factories?"

"Thousands and thousands. In England, for example, by the end of the Second World War, the Royal Air Force had twenty-five thousand women and the number of airplanes produced had risen from two thousand a year to two thousand a month."

"Twenty-five thousand women! How many of them were pilots?"

"Not a single one! In 1925, when they were beginning to establish transport airlines, which meant in concrete terms that at the end of the road there would be not merely glory and death, but also a decent salary, the International Air Navigation Commission decreed that women could not get a commercial pilot's license."

"But didn't the women who already have licenses protest?"

"They were disgusted. All the pioneers, the famous and obscure aviatrixes protested the misogyny and the injustice of it."

"Then what?"

"Deeply impressed by all this shield waving, the International Commission magnanimously granted women the right to obtain a commercial license."

"Too good to be true. What was the catch?"

"A couple of days later, the Commission prohibited the airlines . . ."

". . . from hiring women pilots!"

"Worse—they were prohibited to entrust passengers to women pilots."

"Human lives?"

"Right," Noria said.

"To the same women who had borne their own children!"

"And who had broken all those distance and endurance records, who had crossed the mountain ranges, who had been the stars of their air shows, drawing record crowds, filling their tills. I retain a deep nostalgia for those missing pages in the history of aviation, the pages that relate to those giantesses and their offspring."

"The pages from the pink legend!"

"Pink on a sky-blue background."

"What is the pink?"

"The absoluteness of love," Noria said.

"What love are we talking about?"

"Intelligent love and what is inseparable from it—intelligent sacrifice."

"I have never seen this shocking pink!"

"It sleeps hidden in the splendour of the stars."

"It is inaccessible to most of us . . ."

"But a day will come," Noria assured me, her voice breaking.

She was a victim of a secret universe of those who, devastated by angels or demons, float for long periods to unbind themselves, unwind, and unite with the silence. So that she would not fade away from earth, I went on questioning her.

"Why were flying machines made such symbols of virility?"

"Until 1926, it wasn't easy to gain access to the flying machines. But in 1927, Lindbergh's extraordinary feat closed all the doors to women. What glory to be a pilot in a storm of banners and magnesium flashes. Instant renown! Politicians, statesmen, kings, poets, and writers all suddenly converted themselves into aviators because the press was interested in them and wrote about their exploits. Mussolini had himself photographed in a tri-motor plane which he appeared to be piloting himself. The Italians hailed him as the foremost Italian aviator. Edward VIII of England had himself photographed flying his own plane and, in his imperial way, assured the press that he had his pilot's papers and that, along with hunting, flying was his favourite pastime. In literature, if Saint-Exupéry was flying over Morocco and South America, other writers—D'Annunzio, Malaparte, Cendrars, Malraux—followed his example and replaced the risks of the trade and the apprentice pilots' long hours of training with a frequently inspired lyricism."

"In America, aside from Charles Lindbergh, whom did we have as new heroes?"

"Howard Hughes and Mickey Mouse! Mickey Mouse personally piloted his plane through the skies in the comic strips. Not to be left behind, the Vatican formed a flying missionary group and the very rich Westinghouse Company introduced a new radio set called *Pilot of the Air*."

"We were living and breathing aviation?"

"We grew up in a superterrestrial atmosphere which was announcing the beginning of a new world. And because it was so beautiful, aviation gave us a feeling of moral comfort."

"And the men did not want to share this beauty!"

"Ambition and lust for glory are terrible dictators."

"But what did they finally give as an official reason for not allowing women to transport passengers?"

"They asked women pilots to wait until aviation came to be considered a normal form of transportation worldwide. Only then would they be able to judge on a universal scale the equal merits of male and female pilots."

"They were seen as adversaries."

"Whose competition they had to watch out for."

"They were so extraordinary?"

"Prodigious! They were just a collection of heroic deeds, records boldly broken against time, exhaustion, freezing winds, hurricanes of heat, and fatal fogs. They performed incredible, fearless feats of self-possession to the wonder of all those others who still retained a childlike spirit and disheartened all the rest. In France there were Maryse Bastié, Adrienne Bolland, Hélène Boucher and, a little later on, Jacqueline Auriol and Danielle Décuré. In New Zealand, there was Jean Batten and in Germany, Hanna Reitsche. From the United States, Jacqueline Cochran, Ruth Nichols and Amelia Earhart. In England, Mary Heath, Amy Johnson, and Mary Bailey. In Ethiopia, Moulon Embete and in Canada, Joan Bonnisteel. Nothing stopped them, neither danger by day nor dangers by night.

"In 1920, Adrienne Bolland decided to attempt the Andes cordillero, which no one had so far been able to cross. Adrienne Bolland would accomplish this deed in a plane that was so small and so full of holes that no male aviator would dare fly it over a meadow full of flowers. Convinced that she would never return, her mechanic, with tears in his eyes, gave her a revolver and suggested she commit suicide if she went down in the Andes and did not kill herself in the crash."

"But she made it?"

"She made it," Noria said with a brilliant smile. The Chilean people could not believe their eyes. There was a general pandemonium. They bore the new heroine aloft in triumph. They covered her with cherub's feathers and amulets. They gave her ovation after ovation. She was a saint! A goddess! Descending from heaven, she had soared as high as the huge Andean birds with their puffed-out feathers which forge a passage through the light and clouds. Telephones and telegraphs buzzed, radios crackled, and the next day, all of South America was devouring the details of her exploit in the Santiago Gazette. The article began:

> The humming of the engines woke the condors in their proud nests. The condors were astounded and wondered, "Who dares to fly as high as we?" And the Andes answered, "Don't complain. That is Adrienne Bolland, come from Paris, who is disturbing you."

"They were rivals. They were formidable opponents," I said. "No wonder men were afraid of them."

"And they were feminists to boot! In 1934, Louise Weiss, an internationally known feminist, organized a congress at Bordeaux to demand the vote for women. Those aviatrixes came from all over the world with their planes in support of the extraordinary Louise Weiss, rallying the Air Club and the city airport and bringing this meeting to international attention."

We stayed without speaking for a long time, as on a snowy day. I looked at Noria seated on the sofa beside me. She was only physically present. I could have examined her with X-rays and I would not have seen her. She had gone on the quiet up that silken ladder beyond that unbreachable circle in the ether where we go by night to ask if the realms of glory still remember us. And, reassured, though only just, and comforted, but only just, we come back to earth to fulfill our mission of resurrection through human distress.

Then I felt her presence once again. The ghost had returned.

"In conditions like these, how did women ever learn to fly?"

"Generally by marrying men cut from the same cloth and with the same single-minded desire to fly."

"You want me to believe that the war between the sexes sank without a trace? That everything became simple and uncomplicated?" I said, flaring up.

"There was always pain and conflict," she said, putting her arms around me. "But there was also the pleasure of dreaming of the feats they would accomplish someday and of the glory they perhaps would share."

"I think a woman might just as well receive a deathblow," I said, getting up to sit on a chair.

"Whatever are you talking about?"

"I am talking about that dreadful bond that can exist between a man and a woman . . ."

"I'm too tired to talk about *that*," she said.

". . . and that it's frequently a death threat for both of them," I added, my heart pounding.

A moment later, she went and sat down on another chair.

"I am not predicting the corruption of our civilization," I said.

"I know that . . ."

"Your grandfather was involved in the period of the conquest of the air, wasn't he?"

"For my grandfather and others like him, the baptism of the air was never a sacrament. They abused the situation in a very sinister way to accomplish their own ends."

"What ends were those?"

"Money, power, worship, that emanation from the animal. Populations on their knees! Oh, that they would throw themselves at their feet to embrace their shoes and the corpse-laden earth they stood on," Noria said.

"They were the kind who always know how to turn a situation to their own advantage?"

"Yes, because they were determined to be the shrewdest. They were men of destiny."

"Men of destiny fascinate me . . ."

"They lie flat across our interior landscape like blood on the stage or a lake on the earth."

"A peculiar lake," I said. "Millions of years deep in the centre and so far down that you can never hope to retrieve anyone or anything from it that is still identifiable."

"Blood is the best theatre," said Noria, getting up from her chair in a dizzying movement, a movement filled with light. "After the first shudders of revulsion, we cannot stretch our eyes wide enough to view that bloody flood finally halted. Those hot pulsations and those red connections are part of the past which, beyond death, continue to launch an appeal to life."

"Blood is the most living thing on earth," I heard myself say. The supercharged atmosphere that Noria knew how to create had prompted this response. Once again, she was giving me the impression of trying to surmount the horror of a past act with all her strength and now her body and her mind were in a region where she was neither victim nor executioner.

I took a deep breath before asking if it was primarily money that gave control.

Noria took off her garments of light and fell back into the shadow of that heavy work of reconstruction that I had laid on her.

We were in the Waiting Room. One after another, she handed over morsels of her life.

"You can control through fear even better," Noria said. "It is so easy to incite other people to violence. All you have to do is utter a long, emotional shriek which confuses patriotism, vengeance, and the maniacal pursuit of material wealth."

"Men of destiny are ready to make unlimited sacrifices for their ideals."

"The old peasant virtues of hard work and saving. Order! Authority! Eye for an eye, tooth for a tooth and scream against the emancipation of women and blacks!"

"And your mother's family?"

"The young American middle class," she said with a melancholy smile. "A highly educated family which made themselves heard in the public arena, who wrote newspaper and magazine articles. In my mother's family, they believed in unions and the purity of the working class. America, they wrote, will redress all the wrongs of the old world because she represents future humanity which will share its bread and wine among all the nations of the world. This family wished for stable economic conditions and especially for peace in a world where women would take their place. They believed that when socialism finally broke over America, they would have found the promised land."

"How was it that two people who came from such different backgrounds could have met each other, fallen in love, and married? Explain this mystery to me."

"It was a bad marriage," Noria answered uncompromisingly. "A bad marriage, like so many others."

"But they loved each other, didn't they?"

"Who can say anything that makes sense about one's parents' love and sex life?"

"No one. Our explanations are always based on our own prejudices and preferences."

"There is no clear note to sound."

"The cacophonous orchestra. Burst eardrums. Eros and Thanatos. Oedipus. Adam and Eve. Orpheus and Eurydice. Narcissus. Lilith. Yin and Yang. Mirrors, masks, obsidian stones, axes, and swords. The anguished danse macabre wanders through every hemisphere."

"Just one clear note," Noria repeated in a supplicating voice.

"If we were to hear it, would we recognize it?"

"I would. An uncomprehending life is a dead life," she said with tension in her voice.

"A life of regret is also a dead life," I said, moving toward her.

What we call chance encounters and happy coincidences are miraculous bridges between those who are moving toward each other, I thought. And perhaps it is in this way that we come gradually closer to that cry suspended in the Heavens above our Earth that bids us Love . . . Love!

"Tell me about your father," I said, holding my breath. She looked at me and said nothing. Then she in turn came forward on the bridge. I felt the bump when she took flight by means of fire and pain. With all the strength of her concentrated energy, she wrenched up the words and phrases she had held inside her. Each memory tilted its giant surface and turned on the wing toward the river of dead souls.

"They called him the Lion of Bangor! As a young man, he was famous all over North America for his daring and courage, his physical strength, his beauty and his intelligence. Since the Victorian period, they have been wild about this kind of personality in America. In a society in transition, the gallantry and tenacity with which he endeavoured to reconcile his calling as a doctor with the expression of a kind of romantic nostalgia for the pioneering way of life earned him the sympathy of his elders, the envy of his peers, and the adoration of women. He did everything brilliantly, expressing his mental vigour and his muscular strength. In spring, he could wade up to his hips for hours in the icy waters, depending on the strength and quickness of his legs to avoid being knocked over by chunks of ice coming downstream; he never went back home without catching the biggest trout in the river in the still water below the log dams.

"He loved to ski madly down the most torturous and dangerous slopes in the mountains. Like the Nose Dive trail in Vermont with its seven steep turns and its icy base. One day, in order to extend the amount of skiing time available, he rigged up the first 'mitten-eater' at the base of a steep hill. This was the quaint name he gave to his ropetow, made out of an endless cable and a wheel powered by an old Ford. This invention was a wild success and each weekend, hundreds of skiers would form a queue at the base of the steep hill, hoping to hang onto the mitten-eater which climbed with its winter steps toward the breathing forests of the peak.

"But my father soon lost interest in this invention, leaving to others the pleasure of perfecting and exploiting it, because nothing at all really gripped him except his profession. He asked his own father for a considerable sum of money, all the money necessary to build the most modern medical offices on the East Coast. This sum was not generously forthcoming and in the months that followed, my grandfather spent considerable time reproaching his only son for not pursuing his noble profession.

"My grandfather was a bandit—in financial circles they called him an empire builder. He was ambitious and unscrupulous and, after having acquired, through bankruptcy, several European aviation companies and stolen all the ship-building companies between Portsmouth and Halifax, he had made a fortune. Everyone who did not know him, or who were only slightly acquainted with him respected and admired him. His wife had been dead for a long time. His wife, my grandmother, had gone down off the Azores with one of his yachts, the America II, only a few months after the birth of her son, while on an Atlantic Ocean cruise for her health. My mother used to say that these people were like pallid old gargoyles, in the last stages of becoming human financial rubbish according to her.

"My grandfather's great work came to an abrupt end in the Stock Market crash of 1929. His financial ruin took away that warm, vital Self which he believed, as we all do, to be the centre of the universe. With the American flag carefully folded and tucked under his arm and without leaving any forwarding address, he evacuated his dying soul through the highest window of a Chicago skyscraper.

"The Lion of Bangor did not mourn for his father or at least he didn't seem to. Whatever significance this faint track of a human passing had for him, he meant to pursue his life work as a doctor, as a researcher who shoved aside all those who wore the uniform of the vanquished and who humbly danced in the wake of despair. Didn't his office already welcome the masters of the air and those who sailed the oceans filled with a mad poetry? And those addicted to the snowy solitude of the forests of the New Atlantis? And those nuns tinged with mysticism who claimed to live exclusively on bleeding roses and ecstasy. And those mothers who were exquisitely nervous or filled with icy tremors. All these fragile human bodies came knocking at his office door like a ram inflamed by the springtime.

"They all went on and on in his office. For that was what was agitating them—a compelling hunger for eternity. My body, my mind, my sexual organs want to conquer time, doctor. I am a consumer of eternity. I am a capitalist of the other life!

"The Lion of Bangor generously often treated their wounds and cracks for nothing, giving to the poorest patients the feeling of having received medical treatment usually reserved for kings and queens. And it was true—what he sold to the richest, he gave to the others.

"Very late one summer evening, a slightly dishevelled young woman appeared in his office.

" 'I have heard that you can work miracles with your salve,' " she said, displaying a swollen ankle which he prodded delicately.

" 'You hear a lot of things,' he answered evasively, not even looking at her.

" 'Is it sprained?'

" 'It's a severe sprain,' he said, applying the salve to the contusion.

"His salve was a pungent brown paste which he took from a ceramic jar. He massaged the ankle with a masterful energy.

" 'The pain is much less,' she said, astounded.

" 'In a few minutes, the swelling will go down and your skin will return to its normal colour.'

" 'This must be Good Samaritan salve!' she exclaimed.

"He looked at her.

" 'But you haven't been beaten by thieves,' he answered.

" 'In these violent times . . . ,' she said as she rose slowly.

"She is about to metamorphose into an invisible atmosphere, he thought. He looked at her in the same way you look at a new water source in the springtime.

"'What are you doing with your life?' he asked her tensely.

"'I take care of the dead. I beg for them since they cannot. A few pennies, just a few pennies for something to wrap them in before they are shoved into the mire of a common grave. A few pennies, just a few pennies, and I will sing a hymn of resurrection. But they say a lot of things about my business,' she added ironically.

"They were standing face to face. A magnesium bolt crashed down upon them. They tottered.

"'And what are you doing with your life?' she finally asked. Her sudden voice was worn to a thread.

"'I am slipping myself into the funeral procession,' he heard himself say with amazement. 'I bear healing potions, salves, and cosmic radiations.'

"'You are one of the Fates,' she said. 'When you appear, human pain takes flight. Otherwise . . .'

"'Otherwise, the night is empty,' he said.

"They did not take their eyes off each other. It was as though their pupils were about to burst from this burning vision—love in the glare of its own infinity. The thunderclap made them totter once again.

"Who are you, thunderclap? Do we know your true identity? I suspect you of being the original Father of Tenderness on the earth. I suspect you of sweeping above the world with your power to strike, leaving parallel wounds in our hard bark. And why and for whom is this phenomenal speed? This speeding up of the heart, this vibration in the blood, this sudden perception of secret things? Is it to lighten us who only can walk with a muffled tread, slowly and heavily, through the sands of time?

"She sat down again. She looked at the furnishings in the office. A sober peace tinged with mystery and with a certain degree of asceticism permeated the room. A few lamps illuminated the long wooden tables and the shelves mounted to the ceiling which were crowded, in evident disorder, with implements, jars, test tubes, retorts, a still, microscopes, and some open books.

"'What are you looking for?' she asked.

"'I cultivate cells. I am looking for proofs, the fusion, the mixture, the invisible counterpart of this so-called new fatal illness we now call cancer. I perceive, fleetingly, an extraordinary reality. But now and then, I feel that my brain cells are insufficiently aware to take hold of this reality. And anyway . . .'

" 'And anyway?'

" 'When I see an airplane rising into the sky, I tell myself that we have overcome the law of gravity and that this extraordinary discovery increases human vitality. It puts us in tune with the universe in a new and more intense way.'

"She got up to look at the books in a large bookcase which took up the whole of one wall.

" 'Your books are different from any I have seen before,' she said nervously.

" 'Those books are old, terribly old and filled with what has sustained the rights of the mind, of science, and of culture. The parchment volumes are written in Latin and German,' he added, rubbing his tired eyes. 'They are full of notes, drawings, and chemical and alchemical references.'

" 'What do they say?'

" 'They contain extraordinary stories about human civilizations and their quest for healing and immortality; accounts of what corrupts and what kills. They also contain accounts of that very special automaton, ravenous and often cracked because he abuses his mechanism—the human body. They say that in the very distant past, all of man's energies were centred on the perpetuation and reproduction of the species. That was an appalling time of cruelty and promiscuity, murder, and incest. Those primitive civilizations abused all forms of sexuality for centuries before they were decimated by venereal disease. They gradually disappeared and all the corpses returned to the ground, leaving the germs of horrific diseases in the soil. We are familiar with certain of these diseases, but others, still hidden in the earth, are waiting only for a telluric jolt, a ground swell, or a convenient hurricane.'

"There was such an intensity in his voice and such passion in his tone that she shut the book she had been holding open in her hands and gave him a challenging look.

" 'Is that what you read in these books?'

" 'Some of these books hint at it. But others can be clearly understood if you know how to decode and interpret them.'

" 'Nothing is more difficult than to see things as they really are,' she said.

" 'True enough, if your body and your brain impose narrow limits! But for me, it is a simple question of temperament,' he concluded.

" 'Whenever I hear someone talking about temperament, I am sure they are talking about a psychic deficiency. Temperaments are not simply individual, as they would have us believe. They are racial and national as well.'

" 'You are right,' he said, briskly tapping his foot. 'There is something frightful in each of our temperaments. I am groping and searching,' he added, after a moment.

" 'So am I,' she said. 'There's nothing else to do.'

" 'Every day, before I begin work on culturing cells, I despondently weigh up my mistakes and my lack of depth. If you only knew how insupportably dark human thought is to me!'

" 'To a doctor, whatever deals with sickness and death must be the most profound.'

" 'You speak like an angel,' he said slowly, in a troubled way. 'May I ask you what you are doing in this town? You don't come from here, I know that.'

" 'I am an American made from a little Oregon and Mississippi mud, with some of the perfectly clear desert nights of Baja California added in. A few days ago, I was in Boston,' she said in a changed voice. 'I saw a picture in the paper of a woman who had been found slashed and strangled on the banks of the Penobscot River. She is in the Bangor morgue and no one has claimed her.'

" 'Listen,' he said, taking her hand. 'There are thirty points which permit identification of a corpse—there are always signs, fingerprints, palm prints, dental records, eye and hair colour, surgical scars. I assure you that cadavers can be made to speak, even if they are disfigured or quite decomposed. It's a kind of archaeology.'

" 'She has been in a drawer in the morgue for weeks. Even death has mislaid her name,' she said in a voice so soft and low that the Lion of Bangor's heart contracted.

" 'You are a woman unlike any other,' he said. He turned his eyes to the window, through which Jupiter, the most brilliant star in the evening sky, could be seen.

"'Once in New York,' she said, 'I claimed the body of a woman. She had been in a drawer in the morgue for more than five months. She was all black. We are all black in death. The dead blacken and decompose and, finally, they no longer feel anything, except for soil and fertilizer. In Chicago, Atlanta, Little Rock, Wichita, Denver, Phoenix, in Santa Fe, no one ever claims them. The newspapers publish a photo which never identifies them. Women starved to death! Women frozen to death in the wind and snow. Others maddened to death by racism and sexism. All these women who have gone up in flames in the thick stench of the steel ovens of an economy in crisis. That's the unbreathable stink of cremation.'

"'We are the descendants of so many killers,' he said, making a faint gesture of supplication.

"'In times of crisis or war, just being a woman constitutes an incitement to rape and murder.'

"'I am horrified by what you are telling me.'

"'I think,' she said in a clear, sharp voice, 'that the facts have never supported that pleasant tale we never tire of repeating about the evolution of mankind. Primitive man is still with us and has been for a long time. He is always lurking and running close to the ground, horribly violent and murderous.'

"She got up to leave.

"'Where are you going?' he asked, upset.

"'Back to where I was when I sprained my ankle.'

"'I'll come with you!'

"'I don't think that's possible—or even desirable.'

"'I shall try to convince you,' he said, placing his hand on her arm. 'You are hurt and exhausted and I feel I am involved in it all.'

"'What am I going to do with you?' she said, taking his arm.

"They went to the cemetery. The rain was falling in little drops, a tinkling of bells on the grave of the unknown woman whom she had buried that morning. The air was thick with the scent of honeycombs. He laid a bouquet of wild flowers on the little mound of freshly turned earth.

"'Are you a father?' she suddenly asked.

"He heard his heart beating, felt an overwhelming sensation of lightness, a stripping away of his entire being as if everything that had been stagnant in him was falling to his toes and taking away his pain and fear. A flood of tenderness and vulnerability opened up a new channel in him.

" 'Sometimes I feel a powerful radiation run through me,' he said happily.

" 'Oh, I know,' she said, 'a ray of energy. And then?'

" 'Then we know nothing bad can happen to us. We know we are protected by life's strength and pity.'

"She began to weep quietly.

" 'When this ray strikes me,' he said, wrapping her in his arms, 'I hear a little girl's voice coming from far, far away. It is as though . . . as though she is speaking to me by means of this radiant energy.'

"Fourteen months later," Noria said, getting up, "I was in the arms of my father, the Lion of Bangor."

"What did you really feel about your father?" I cried out, despite myself.

She did not speak. Her expression was beautiful and dead at the same time.

"I was only a few hours old when he bent over me with his intense smile. First, I was curious. Then I was afraid that this beast with his energy would absorb me and I screamed. I howled! The loneliness which comes about in adulthood or old age, is only a pale recollection. There is nothing like that feeling of loneliness which we experience at the moment we are born on earth."

Fourth Song

These tears from the brooks which water the fields of immortal charity.

H.P. Blavatsky, The Voice of Silence

The places that we live are still permeated with those ancient, little-known, or long-forgotten healing energies which the New Atlantis harbours in its flanks, and so the red cicadas' territory and the Appalachian trail provided a favourable ground for that enterprise of salvation and compassion which was about to become the best and the most important work in the world for us. In a moment of comprehension which imprinted itself on me, I saw certain constructive and protective old souls coming forward among us, to help us collect our separate individualities into a single active force.

These precious old ancestors, great and strong, as numerous as leaves on the trees, know nothing of failure or fear of loss. The anguish of death and the agony of anxiety are wholly foreign to them. Every earthly night, each eternal night, listening only to the loveliest note struck by desire, they alchemically enter every living form, providing a marvellous consolation to those who will go under by autumn's end and revealing to others—those who hesitate, those who are afraid—the exact amorous vibration which gives birth to fruit and flower with a single ray of sunshine.

Afterwards, the red cicadas and I often evoked the striking apparition of the little plane over the flats.

"The airplane enlivened the whole sky with its radiant fabric," the old guard said.

"Something has stayed with us from that single instant when, for once, we were all plugged into the same etherial wavelength."

"Everybody except Jeanne!"

"I object—I was there, but I didn't say a word."

"Not a word? You stayed out of the way by the side of the pond with your lips shut. It seemed as if you were going to stay there for the rest of your life."

"I had a feeling it was dreadful," said someone else, sketching a benediction in the air.

"As dreadful and as beautiful as a birth," I said, feeling joy rising in me. "I saw, I believe, the essence of this distant birth—the airplane rolling across the bent grass, the pilot finally setting her feet on the ground."

"We approached the airplane the way you approach a thought," the old guard said. "Noria looked at us."

"The way you look at something that will determine your fate."

"It was just before nightfall," someone said.

"Rain was rattling in our faces, on the grass, and on the fuselage," someone else said. "Rain is a living reality which spreads over dying souls."

"She took the first crate out," I said.

"I thought something was moving in the bottom of the crate," someone said.

"Not a leaf was stirring on the trees," the other one said.

"She took out a second crate, then a third," I said.

"She put the three crates on the ground at our feet. Then we thought we had rights over these boxes," the old guard said. "We're old and crafty!"

"Now, wait," one said. "She placed the three crates at our feet, exactly at the radiation point of terror."

"What did you hope to find in those boxes?"

"Who knows! Brightly coloured butterflies, tonics, escape powders."

"A simple no-risk way to make a fortune—a safe smuggling route."

"Then," another one remembered, "we would finally lead lives of luxury and enjoy such splendid things—be adventurers, explorers, or pirates—no matter how feeble, we were all ready for action."

"We were all fifty, sixty, seventy years old, Jeanne; we didn't have enough guts to attempt an impossible escape or get false identification. There is no better way to pass the time among old friends and lovers than to dream at home when the rain is falling on the slaty roofs. We're too old and too smart."

"And then you looked in the boxes," I said.

"We saw three animals in the form of a pile of blood," the

old guard said, in a single breath, as if their voices had deserted them.

"What did you think?"

"I thought, what can stop this? What is the magic word to make this stop?"

"I thought that we were living in the final days of this epoch and that we human beings were the authors of all misery and horror."

"I thought of burying my face in these animals and I thought of going far, far away."

"I thought of punishment, sacrifice, immolation and purification."

"I thought of veiling my face, covering my head with ashes and lamenting."

"I thought of all the poisons we had spread."

"I thought of duality."

"I thought of the manifest worlds."

"I thought of revenge."

"I thought that I had already lived through this."

"I thought of pardon," the last of the red cicadas said.

"But you, Jeanne, you stayed down by the pond, cold as the snow."

"Your immobility ate into us. It seemed as though you were having a horrifying perception of us. Had we become dangerous?"

"Yes, maybe. No. Certainly not," I said, softly, conscious that our friendship could evaporate at that very moment, and it would be my fault, my fault, my most grievous fault.

"Do you know," the old guard said, with an indefinable emotion, "that your behaviour bothers us? It's true that friendship between us has never been easy, as if it were connected to you only by a thread. We've asked ourselves—if friendship slips away, can it be held on to at any cost? Can the effort be made to find the words, the gestures which will maintain this friendship in the material fact of our journey in the New Atlantis?"

Tears came to my eyes, tears of guilt and remorse, and tears of love. Embarrassed, I wiped them away with the back of my hand.

"After all, we thought, you are a writer, a woman who leads a quasi-monastic existence. You are a woman who spends hours and hours thinking and writing about the links between living things and the loving call which perhaps determines the time and the place of our birth, and whatever follows. We are probably a little simple, but we imagine you seeing endless visions in dazzling mirrors, from which you draw dizzying perceptions of persons and things. Every day you put yourself at the service of your talents. Whereas for us, we have the sense of falling back into a pursuit of objects which may be desirable but are of doubtful necessity."

"My dear old friends," I answered, almost in tears. "We are not merely friends of one short day. We are friends from long, long ago. The essence of our friendship may date back to the beginning of the world. Through time, cycles, and new beginning after new beginning, this friendship has become richer and richer. It gives us a broad and beautiful perspective of recognition and affection. I believe, from the bottom of my heart, that it is these old friendships which lend a little dignity to our lives."

I saw some expressions lighten and others darken. The old guard was lost in thought. The memory of friendship is erased so quickly, I thought. Some smoke, a little wisp of smoke and nothing more. For most of us, the memory is a funeral pyre which needs constant stoking. And so every memory, every trace, is destroyed. Even the smoke disappears from the mind, sucked up by the present moment and by the ingratitude which disintegrates and disperses the essence of those great memories of sadness and joy.

"The time has come when I am afraid of you," I said.

"Fears draw water from all kinds of springs," the old guard said. "Why are you afraid of us?" she continued, making the questioning in her very low, soothing, interior voice vibrate.

"I have to ascend time," I said. "If I stay in the present, anything at all points to the presence of my fear."

"Tell us. What are you afraid of? Do you think you are going to kill us?" one said.

"It's a long story. I don't know if there's any killing in it. Some years ago, I began a long and lovely detour through the artistic condition. In those days. I wanted to become a virtuoso writer, and I prayed to the powers: *Do you still love me? Answer me; I know you are there! Are my readers dreaming of me?* And so on, praying with my eyes wet, fooling around with my rough drafts, my papers, and my reviews. One day, the spell was broken—exhausted and depressed by the frenzy of my life, I decided to have a real spring cleaning.

My own little personal revolution! An irresistible attraction to autonomy.

"Until then, I had never lived by myself. I was convinced that I would know how to look after myself from now on, so, with an enthusiastic wielding of my broom and mop, I swept the slave drivers which had been dominating me—sex, money, ambition—out the door. Then I fired all the old demons who had been manipulating me through fear, pain, and the agony of anxiety. And the last step was to push out the cruellest and most egotistical demons—the ones who beat me black and blue to get me to approach the cult of art and its so-called miracles. That left me with my guilty conscience."

"But you were free," the old guard said.

"I never stopped thinking about them. Were they going to miss me? I had loved burying myself deep inside them. This fear only lasted a while and was replaced by another thought—that my slave drivers had burrowed into me in the opposite direction and would haunt me for the rest of my days."

"They didn't burrow into you," someone said.

"They remained out there to suffocate with rage and rot on the spot. Have you never heard the cries of birds of prey and seen their circling shadows skimming over that stench?" someone else said.

"If you say so!"

"Ancient human wisdom says so. So you found yourself alone together with your Catholic conscience?" the old guard asked. "The one which has made us believe that a large part of Hell would be reserved personally for us? Is it really filthy down there?"

"Filthy? It is a larval world with squalor in every corner of it. You could cut the air with a knife, as the expression goes, from my guilty conscience and my fear of the eternal darkness. More and more often, I awoke from my own little night, sweating, in tears, and shaking and trembling all up and down my back. And a pack of Great Northern wolves hot on my heels. I felt as though my dreams were punishing me! Another time, I would come back purified, having withstood obstacles and overcome tests. In my sleep, I received visions, I perceived wild voices chanting resonant and towering chants in a fundamental note which eluded me because I lacked the organs which would permit me to hear them and to vibrate along with them. I was wandering in a new world where nothing was what it was. I felt I was a coward, that my cowardice was unparalleled. Insensitive skins brushed by me. Someone stripped me of my flesh. I was taken apart limb by limb and judged. The acts I had committed in my life were weighed—the pure ones marked with white pebbles, the impure with black. When I awoke, I literally woke from the dead. There was only one thing I wanted to do—to get dressed and go out to walk along the Appalachian trail."

"Now that's what I would call evidence of sound good sense. The night air revitalizes us in the mountains."

"Your dreams were the work of some forgotten slave driver," another one said.

"That's what I thought. A forgotten devil I'd been fattening up in my murky depths."

"Who can face up to the enormous needs of the soul?" said the old guard, talking among themselves. "You do what you can and that's all."

"One night," I said, "I woke up after a dream like that. It seemed so real that I ran outside and flew with my arms outstretched toward the smoke rising from your chimneys. I was about to knock on the first door I came to to ask for a little comforting when I heard alarming noises pouring through the walls of your houses. Someone was moving furniture . . . someone was hitting, there were stifled cries of pain . . . a woman was beating another woman, gagging her mouth to keep her from suffering out loud . . . I did not know what to make of this suffering and I felt so close to the scene, just on the other side of the door. Something still lived in me in this region of cruelty and brutality. I fled."

"It is so comforting to be one of those who have been spared," one of them said, in a voice which sank to the depths of the earth.

"The world is full of extremely tactful people who don't want to know," said another one. "I suppose you must have a grudge against us," another added fervently.

"A grudge? Right then, I hated you the same way one might hate whoever violates one's most cherished secret, whoever is disgusted by one's cowardice. I was vulnerable in such a mean and petty way . . ."

"It is not always the lofty obstacles which make us trip so often in our rescue missions or which keep us from transforming ourselves and the world as much or as well as we might," one of them said.

"The finest plans in our lives fail for the most insignificant and petty reasons," said someone else.

"After I fled, I thought about you all night long," I said. "I had believed that you possessed a collective plan and vast aims . . ."

"But you never, never imagined that there were those among us who were cruel and spiritually underdeveloped!"

"I had my insights and my inspirations. I hope that the age of inspiration will never be a thing of the past," I said.

"Oh, inspiration, intuition," the old guard murmured, with a shudder which could have reached the sun. "Without those, we are as powerless as a child in its parents' arms. Without them, how can we think about higher things?"

"Without them, can we be sheltered from being ambushed by despair?"

"Inspiration and intuition are essential, but are ideals?"

"I had an ideal vision of all of you, but I have sacrificed it," I muttered.

I had barely pronounced these words when I felt once more the impact of takeoff. The magic plane plucked me from the ground and bore me away, just before sunrise, toward a region resonating with the vast silence of an invisible presence. When that happens to you, a superior instinct makes you understand that you will taste a rare, rare joy—the joy of recovering intact that memory of immortality which you encounter in your dreams. With a queenly ease, you will leap from peak to peak with the centaurs and fly through the constellations with the wild geese and swans.

"Have you never tried to get control over yourselves?" I asked the old guard.

"That's a false direction," they answered angrily. "That's foam. Here we are in the process of becoming. After having sounded the rallying trumpets to the communal life, each of us returned to her previous stony existence. The need to be of service to others admitted no weakness."

"You are presenting yourselves in a disturbing light."

"An outside, powerful force urged us to believe we were unique, different, heroic," the old guard said angrily.

"We thought we were superior to the rest of humanity," one of them said, pressing her hand to her breast as though she wanted to wring her heart and then wrench it. Out of modesty, she did not rend her heart and her hand, falling away, rested on my shoulder after having ruffled my hair.

"A genuine communion was established between ourselves and this powerful force. This force stuck to us and we could hear its footsteps in our sleep. Then, at one point, some of us felt impelled by an irresistible need for scholarship," the old guard said. "Sheltered, surrounded by books, they began to explore a gold mine which they thought would be inexhaustible, piling up the strangest bits of knowledge about animate matter, about the bloody rot and darkness of human civilizations. Others, feeling themselves drawn by the scented outdoor air, were surrounded by endless care and concern from the flowers, the trees, and the grass of our territory."

"So some of you spent your lives in a distant slumber while others, if sometimes perplexed, sought energetically and courageously for that form, that beautiful form of expression or of essential orientation their lives might take when the proper moment arrived."

"That's about what we thought. Yes, Jeanne, we wanted to be the agents of our own destiny," another one said.

"That will to change gave us wings—until a violent wind came and shook us about."

"The universal spirit of aggression—ideological quarrels, threats, blackmail, cruelty—it was as though our thoughts contained only the dregs of carnage and tortured flesh," someone said.

"It played itself out in the shadows," said someone else. "Oh, the Shadow! The Shadow no one speaks of. It is always there, nevertheless. You don't see it, that's all. Is it an animal? To some degree. Is it a human being? Always. Does it move as we move? Yes, it does."

"To listen to you, one would think that the Shadow is more terrifying than the unknown," I said.

"It is the most fertile seed on our entire planet," one of them said. We are part of those who beat and those who are beaten. In the Shadow!"

"The most odious and horrible secrets of human history throb powerfully in the Shadow," said someone else.

"And supposing it was all a mirage, an insignificant fact. Or supposing you were all a bit mad? Obsessive," I added, forcing a simple, casual smile.

"From now on, the Shadow and the Light are no longer in simple opposition," one said in a voice warmed with the flame of conviction. "For the first time in history, the Shadow, confronted by the Light, draws back."

"And you believe that this will reverse the course of things? The Shadow has watched over us very well."

"It is in our brains like an abscess," the old guard said in a voice moved by grief. "The history of civilization and the stories of each of our own lives are tales of the Shadow. The Shadow has forever woven the Atmosphere of the Age—it gives rise to that general atmosphere which is so dark, heavy, sad, and inconceivably dispiriting. The Shadow is that warehouse where we conceal our dirty thoughts and our bad deeds. All human misery is hidden there, possessed by passion and pride."

"I want to be saved!" I cried, almost despite myself. "From the Shadow, from cosmic evil, from the terror . . ."

"The whole world wants to be saved." someone said.

"Everyone wants to be saved and everyone loves being saved," said someone else. "Is it a sacred need? Is it a comforting thought which does not involve our immediate responsibility?"

"When we were bent over Noria's boxes, over those three animals in the form of a pile of blood," the old guard continued in a faint voice, "we were taking deep breaths of unbreathable air, the Atmosphere of the Age. It is opaque, it gets in everywhere, it is the Atmosphere of the Age which gives rise to that mental atmosphere filled with screams of horror and suffering from all those twitching beasts we massacre in our slaughterhouses, which we coldly and scientifically mutilate and torture in our laboratories."

"Don't forget the love of sport," I said. "That organized slaughter called hunting and fishing. Where do those shrieks of pain and terror go?" I asked, close to fainting.

"Those cries of loathing for the entire human race? There they are. They slip like shadows into the air we breathe. They mingle with the rain, they crackle in the fire, they descend in the fog," one of them said.

"There isn't enough clean air," said another one. "Unless you destroy the cosmic stuff which envelops the universe. The general atmosphere is an occupied zone filled with the enormous hordes of animals we have assassinated and this fetid air multiplies all our feelings of aggression, cruelty, and guilt by ten."

"I know a country where hunting and fishing are viewed as crimes," I said. "Where love and devotion flow between the animal and the human realm like a river into the sea. In Tibet, killing or even wounding the smallest creature is an evil and the sin is judged a particularly grave fault when the fish are little and a number have to be killed to make an adequate meal. They say that small and large creatures in this country have no fear of humans. You can pet a hare and the birds perch on your shoulder."

"Alas, that is not enough. The minimal number of animals we allow to die in peace is quickly absorbed by the hordes of our victims all shuddering with hatred for their torturers," the old guard said. "When we bent over those animals, we knew that our cruelty drew the most repulsive stench in the universe down over us."

"Something hovered in the air," one said. "It might have been a spark from an encounter with compassion. Perhaps we have now finally discovered our usefulness on earth."

"It is the spark from our star," the other said.

"What is that star called?"

"It sometimes happens that the tail of the comet Berenice, unwinding in its sleep, hides it from our sight," someone said, in a voice strangely calm.

"But in what quarter of the night does it shine?" I insisted.

"It spends its most beautiful hours in the constellation Virgo," said the other one in a voice that had no desire to conceal anything.

"It sounds as if Virgo would change you into pillars of salt or trap you in the bowels of time!"

"The stars arrange and dispose themselves in so many ways in their route of abundance," someone said.

"Our star is called Spica. That means 'Blade of Wheat'. It signifies the nourishing and protection of every living thing in every realm. You can see it in the east through your window," the old guard said. "It rises and sets in silence and pours itself out in the invisible."

"For how long has it hung over this zone?"

"It is in its early childhood," one said, in a slow voice. "It's hardly two thousand years old. The Zodiacal archives relate that at that time, Saturn and Jupiter abruptly entered into a conjunction in the sign of Pisces with Sirius, the brightest of the seven stars in the Great Bear which was boiling, immense, in the south. When this conjunction of stars occurred in the night, something new put down its roots in the sky. An Oriental astrologer had the luck to see the Blade of Wheat spilling a flood of sun over a little village whose name, in Hebrew, means, 'The House of Bread.'

"What is the Hebrew name of this village?"

"Bethlehem," one said.

"The Blade of Wheat appeared in the sky the night before Christmas," the other one said.

"What did this appearance mean?"

"It meant that all our ancient tears of pain, the ancient tears buried alive in the human race, were about to be reborn. At last, life would take a new surge and experience an evolutionary thrust . . ."

"Would all living creatures evolve, or just those who are human?" I asked.

"The development of whatever bears a human face. The development of whatever bears an animal face. In this new night, an accelerated development of certain animal species which we had already begun to domesticate in Asia and Europe was anticipated. It was foreseen that these animals—the cat, the horse, the dog, the elephant—would become more and more devoted to humans. A new spirit awakened on the earth," the old guard said.

"I've not been seeing very clearly," one said, raising her voice to show that what would follow was addressed to us all. "Why do we have this obsession with our collective destiny? Why choose to limit ourselves? Why have we not bowed our old faces to the ground and made our lament? Why have we made a negative energy out of this zodiacal sign of our age, this magnificent constellation of Virgo entering into eternity two thousand years ago?"

"At one time, we were in touch with such greater dimensions of existence. But we drew back. We refused to evolve. Why? Why?" the old guard demanded.

"We have come back from there marked with the seal of anguish," another said, grasping my hand.

"Once," I said, "I was in touch with much vaster dimensions.

I thought at once that it was by pure chance if I, Jeanne, were touched by an equally lovely emanation. I felt the need to retreat to recover as quickly as possible the same spiritual state I had been in before."

"Our experience is just as you have described. Why this refusal? Why?"

"I don't know if I have a satisfactory answer," I said. "More and more human beings are coming to recognize that only a knowledge of the invisible will permit them to go forward and save their souls. Under the powerful effect of this desire, they advance, they evolve, and suddenly . . ."

"They stop, turned to stone! However, that was only the voice of the Shadow muttering his sentences of exile and death," the other one said. "That was only the voice of the Guardian of the Threshold, singing his spellbinding music."

"There is yet another factor," I added. "This refusal is, I think, grounded in a universal sense of fear—the fear of not being up to the opportunity being offered to us."

"Noria and her animals," one said happily. "The opportunity which only knocks once, perhaps. We recognized it and took advantage of it."

"The time spent gazing at the stars was not time lost," another said.

"All the great texts of the past allow us to journey under the vault of heaven, where the races of humanity no longer measure the span of their existence in a constantly narrowing life or in what they throw away. Women and men, generation after generation, follow the ascending path of souls which crosses the twelve signs of the Zodiac. The same descending path awaits our birth. The word *zodiac*, from the Greek *zodion*, means 'little animal'."

"The Zodiac is the circle of starry animals," the old guard said. "It is our celestial eyes."

Noria's arrival was like a sign of destiny along the Appalachian trail. There are innumerable paths leading us from where we are through pain, doubt, and despair to compassion for all that exists.

It was already the end of October and the hunters were hunting, slaughtering the wild ducks flying toward the south in meagre flocks. Over the mountains, the Canada geese, their wings beating in majestic rhythms, passed, calling *farewell, farewell*. Noria was flying in the opposite direction, climbing the cold currents of air with her sparkling wings and her passengers, the dogs, only dogs, barely identifiable in their doggy essence, bent shadows devoured by suffering.

"Where did they come from?"

"From New England. From university and drug company labs, those pinnacles of mutilation and the secret struggle of agonized animals," Noria said.

"Why so many dogs?"

"Because dogs are more resistant than any of the other victims. The surgical experimenter prefers dogs. The most ham-fisted or incompetent vivisectionist can succeed in cutting up a dog without killing it. Since 1945, around a billion dogs have been tortured to the point of death."

"A billion mutilated phantoms whose shrieks of hatred for the human race haunt the Atmosphere of the Age! I am overcome."

"Do turtles dream?" Noria asked, in a voice swaddled in white.

"Sea turtle, land turtle, messenger from beyond, tortoiseshell comb, do you dream?"

"How many have died?"

"Eighteen million turtles dead with electrodes buried in their brains. For monkeys, rabbits, cats, mice, and calves, the figure of six billion is conservative," Noria said.

On the Appalachian trail, we bind the wounds, we nurse, we console. There are dogs whose skin is rolled back to the bone. The nerves, the tendons, and the muscles are visible. They still contract in the infernal heat of pain.

Despite all our care, the skeletal bitch on whom they had perfected a variety of weight-reduction diets died. She was a beagle. We called her Anna.

The dog under whose skin the psychopaths from the laboratory had sewn a fifth paw also died. Robert, the Beauce Shepherd, once capable of running dozens of kilometres a day, and of guarding our flocks and our homes. Able to protect us, to drive back our enemies with his fine black gaze. Able to love us to the end. With his fifth paw, Robert, that "country gentleman," as Colette put it, knew he was a dog in exile. One morning, he lay his coat down in the dew and began his death moan. The grief in his expression overwhelmed everything and opened great frightening veins. He wanted no more of this non-life. We were with him to the end . . . you understand . . . the final release . . . that planetary nausea which tears the tortured body and runs deeper than the earth to expose its excrement, blood, and breath. Indignant tears veiled our eyes. Is there any way to make up for this? To protest, shoulder to shoulder? Then came the moment of truth. That moment of sincerity which is so brief, so shocking among human beings, that moment which is so moving among animals because it expresses the truth of an entire life.

The old guard often put an end to a dog's suffering with an injection. We would bury them in the shadow of a birch tree, a cedar, or a little love maple.

Someday, perhaps tomorrow, the return will occur. That precious old ancestor will return who, long, long ago, imagined us in a luminous perspective, like a possible ideal.

But some of the dogs survived. These dogs were afraid of everything. They were suspicious of unfamiliar visitors. They trembled and hid themselves for hours. They disappeared. They went through walls and doorways and returned to lie at our feet, out of breath from having run across the prairies of the other world. Our dogs could hardly bear to look a human being in the eyes. Noria said that was because they were afraid of the cruelty or indifference they might find there. Some dogs did survive. By a miracle!

Only One-Eye is an example. The little Pekinese had been bound to an operating table in a stress experiment described as elegant and classic by scientific investigators the world around. She was to get electric shocks to the heart until death ensued. To what end? To demonstrate that it requires less electricity to electrocute a dog under stress than a dog that is relaxed!!! The amphitheatre was filled to bursting. At the moment that the experiment was about to proceed, the professor noticed a trickle of blood in one empty eye socket. "Gentlemen," he said to the students, "it appears that one of my colleagues needed an eye." This remark was greeted with general hilarity in the amphitheatre. "I refuse," he added, "to interrogate this dog under these conditions." There was another burst of laughter from the students when the experimenter demanded someone bring him a dog under less stress. The little Pekinese was abandoned, dying, on a cart.

"She ought to have died on that cart from pain and affliction," Noria said, stroking Only One-Eye's coat and clasping her in her arms.

"Her broken heart went on beating."

"Someone took pity on her. From life to life, everywhere on earth, there is always more pity and more compassion."

"Everything we can give is still far from enough," I said. "But the torturers do not work all by themselves. I feel I am their accomplice at the other end of the tunnel. They are, as I am, the result of the past."

"No one could call you inhuman or insensitive," Noria protested.

"Am I not, like them, bound to the earth? Am I not possessed of passions and desires? And a lot of other feelings which disgust me so much that I dare not look at them too closely?"

"That is because you are looking into the mirror of the past. A pit! However, we are at last sailing on the waters of the future. Of course, we are taken unawares by the acceleration of time."

"That's utopian! We are still in the waters of the past. The poor sick souls who practice this persistent and deliberate cruelty constantly return among us with the intention of dragging us, one more time, down the path they are on themselves."

"Their influence is rapidly declining," Noria whispered and closed her eyes.

"It is such a long road. I am with you from the bottom of my heart. We are old, dying souls," I added, and closed my eyes as well.

"We are ripening so slowly . . ."

"One part of us is wandering in a silent night with its criminal mind and its power to wound. Someday, can we not stop time and the clocks?"

"Why?" Noria said, making a slight movement.

"So we can weep in peace for our folly and our shame," I said.

"But don't you see that this is a time of greatness! Can't you hear the new heart pulsing as it descends to the Earth?" Noria cried, making a motion which went beyond the living room of our house on the Appalachian trail. Her motion passed between the clouds of snow and continued all the way to Sirius and further still, right to the feet of the Angels of the Presence, to where there is no further bloodshed and no more secrets.

I see Noria collapse.

Responding to an invisible signal, her spirit dives into a feverish lake of inky black. Then her body bends, trembling like a magician's wand.

In a lightning-quick vision, I see her advance to the brink of death, surrounded by a pearly light. She falls to the floor, my inexplicable sister, sister of flesh and resurrection.

I call the town doctor. I call the old guard. I know, however, that there is nothing to be done.

"She isn't putting up a fight," the doctor says as he listens to her heart.

"Help her, I beg of you. She hasn't enough energy left to resist the fever."

"It seems like indifference. It seems like an attempt against life," the doctor repeats, nodding his head.

"What about the hospital . . . intensive care?"

"It's out of the question. She wouldn't get there alive," he says and snaps shut his leather bag.

After the doctor leaves, the old guard says, "Bring her bed close to the window. Today the light is finally breaking through the dome of the clouds. The mountains have never been so beautiful . . ."

We stay at her bedside in silence. We listen to time passing, we hear Noria leaving and with her, the essence of our existence. Are those who are dying still alert to the illumination from the earth and from the immense growth of all that comes and all that goes?

The old guard takes its leave at the hour when the birds no longer sing. This is the first night.

On the third day, someone is knocking at the door. Since a part of me has been living in constant fear, without a break, I am startled. The windows are somewhat misted over and half-covered with snow, but I manage to make out the outline of a car. The thick snow must have muffled the sound of the engine.

I open the door—with his white hair and fine white beard he looks like a resurrected soul whom someone has condemned to walk among the children of the earth for a fixed length of time.

The notion I had of him shatters into a thousand fragments, to be replaced by another which is at once strange and familiar to me.

"You are the Lion of Bangor!"

"And you are Jeanne," he says in a voice which sounds in my ears in all its absolute quality—a funeral knell marking both the fleeting moment and forever.

The entire image I had of him, his authority, will, his ambition, is going by the boards and what is left of the Lion of Bangor has wings.

He is looking shyly around at the things in the house. He bends to pat Only One-Eye's head and Rimouski-Belle questions him by placing her narrow paw in his hand.

"How is my little girl?" he calmly asks.

"She is departing little by little. Every day she goes further away."

"I saw your doctor earlier . . ."

"What is causing all of this?"

"Death."

"The world is inundated with death," I say, trying not to scream.

"The world is inundated with visions," he says, and places his doctor's bag on the floor near the door.

"Who remembers them?" I mutter tensely.

"Those who are left exhausted and shaken by them."

"They leave me in a state of icy calm . . ."

"And gasping? That depends . . ."

"Depends on whom? Depends on what? Do you have the courage to go and wage war in there?" I say, pointing at Noria's room. "Your daughter is just a pile of shadows under a big white sheet. But she is still my entire life," I say, defying him. "My soul sister, as the expression goes. The one whom you never betray and who journeys with you all the way to the moment of salvation or damnation."

Is he shocked, saddened, or disgusted? In any event, he is not giving anything away. He is coming closer to lay an arm around my shoulder. With his giant's steps he is leading me into the room. We are looking at her who will soon be just a rotted thing under the white sheet.

He is bending his broad face over his daughter. He is wiping the drops of sweat from her brow and enfolding his child's hands. I close my eyes so as not see anything more. What good does that do? Even with my eyes shut, I can see the whole thing! He is collecting his thoughts and walking through the fires of a distant childhood, till he bleeds, till he weeps. In silence. In the peculiar light of this aerial space, he is weeping silently so as not to disturb his daughter's apparently peaceful death bed. I am thinking about all those other tearful egoists with their dramatic shrieks and noisy lamentations which assault the dying.

What links me to him is his silence. All at once, by his mere presence, he has transcended the commonplace setting of this Waiting Room.

Later, when I open my eyes, it all continues to happen viscerally. The Lion of Bangor is standing in front of the window. He is looking out at the dazzling white birches and the Royal Road of the Appalachian trail.

"The beauty of this incomparable day." He is thinking out loud and turns abruptly toward me in a sweet and familiar way which adopts me and includes me in his thoughts.

In her bed, Noria, my aerial treasure, is bathed in an alien light.

We are sitting across from one another. A few minutes ago he ate a little bread, a bunch of grapes. He drank a cup of black coffee. Each of his motions makes me feel he thinks it an honour to be eating at my table. He has his daughter's mouth—broad and chiselled. It is a loyal mouth which would not snatch the bread from his neighbour's lips. A mouth which would never bark. I feel both comfortable and comforted in the presence of this magnificent, desolate man. Did I, once upon a time, follow in his wake, somewhere other than America, somewhere other than the earth? Someone murmurs to me *Yes, yes, Jeanne, you have such a short memory*. So, if that is the case, why are we meeting one more time? This time, will we part forever, blessing one another? Or will we leave, cursing each other, to make another appointment?

I do not take my eyes off him. I begin to understand that he is there, across from me, because of the simple fact of the condition I represent, just as I am across from him because of the simple fact of the condition he represents. And so we are alike in this long-lasting maternal realm of births, deaths, and resurrections.

"Oh, I can hear it so clearly! Do you hear it?" he says, his hands in the pockets of his well-worn, very large, tweed jacket.

"Who? Noria? The howling from the city of the dead?"

"No! The song! The song!" the Lion of Bangor repeats.

"It is only the wind singing," I say, shivering.

"The wind does not sing a song, it carries it. That is the song sung by all that is dead and all that is alive. It is composed of the single powerful sound of the loving words that are said in heaven and on earth."

"You are an enigma. Your daughter is an enigma."

"And you are an aristocrat," he says, smiling his first smile at me. "The writer's profession has had its letters patent for a long, long time."

"And so has yours."

"But mine is a violent profession. All we see is filth and fear, aberrations and wounds. It is a calling which too often drives us to indifference toward other people's pain. It makes some of us cynical, greedy individuals, whose pockets are stuffed with the money they have snatched or swindled."

"You paint a gloomy picture," I say. "To me, my profession is full of misdirections and death sentences."

"So why do you do it?"

"Why do you?"

"I don't practice they way I used to. Now I try to pass on the best that is in me."

"I don't have your strength. When you believe that everything is meaningless, your work is still some comfort. You see, I am just corrupt enough to silence my scruples."

"Do you see me as an opponent?" the Lion of Bangor is asking.

"One revelation destroys another. You will never be able to enter my heart."

"I will if you consent to it," he says, returning at the speed of sound.

"Consent to it?"

"It is difficult to consent. You have to be free!"

"And ready to assume total responsibility for all your deeds, for all your cruellest actions, with no one responsible but yourself."

"You are capable of doing that!"

"I am not capable of it!" I say in a panic.

I suddenly have the feeling I am bathing in black, soapy water.

"You are on the verge of a breakdown," he adds. "It is almost inevitable."

"Inevitable? Like your being here?"

My own eyes bloodshot, my face spiteful, I see through his eyes how tortured my words are.

"I am a rolling stone which never comes to rest," the Lion of Bangor is saying desperately.

"I am too full of compassion for myself. I don't have any left over for you!"

"Why do you paint such a morally dark picture of yourself?"

"Because I am unable to love. Though I do believe and hope that love exists."

"Didn't you provide love and hospitality to my daughter with no thought of personal gain? Nothing made you do that . . ."

"That was an egotistical gesture, a gross, impure affection. I prostitute everything to literature," I say with a cold smile.

"Jeanne, Jeanne," the Lion of Bangor repeats, bending almost imperceptibly.

"You know entirely too much! Tell me, how long have you been spying on us? Are you a Supercop, always on the job? How long have you been roaming around our houses?"

"If I roam around, it's with a bell around my neck. Nothing else. There's nothing up my sleeve. Someone has burnt all my uniforms."

"Who has?"

"Life."

"But you still have teeth, fists, and feet." I say. "And words."

"You are looking at my words and gestures through the distorting mirror of your own community."

"My lesbian community?"

"Yes," the Lion of Bangor answers without hesitation.

"At last, we've finally got to it," I say with a sigh of mingled disappointment and relief.

"You're not there at all!"

"I've come to the wrong conclusion?"

"Why should your community distort more than any other? Mine is just as bad."

"But doesn't every social circle drink its fill from an ocean of shared, communal experience?"

"Certainly. As long as they are relatively simple experiences and repeated time and time again."

"When is it ever any other way? For example, whenever are events and the individuals who carry them inside themselves not involved in the landscape of familiar experience?"

"All the time. That's the hell of it. We crush and we are crushed. Someday we will find another means of dealing with good and evil. Who maintains that the imagination is like the madwoman in the attic?" the Lion of Bangor says, his eyes swollen with fatigue. "The real madwoman in the attic is the reason, endlessly tormented by thoughts coming from all over. Some of these thoughts come from the other world, like a passing population. Others, visiting from higher regions, confuse our cerebral and cervical waves. Then, there is that mass of ordinary thoughts, family, social, racial thoughts . . . Oh, how heavily they weigh on us. They suffuse our intelligence. They excite us and skew every proportion; with no opposition at all they lead us to dubious conclusions."

"Now I know," I say, with my eyes fixed on him, and then stop.

"What do you know?"

He is breathing harder. He takes my hand in his trembling hand and leans forward, his great face burning.

"I know that you would never, never, seek to destroy or weaken the feeling which binds us to one another . . ."

"The impulse which presses us toward each other is not phenomenal. It is the highest flight that human beings are capable of on earth."

I am seeing an angel pass by, with its head turned to the rear and its wings folded. It is climbing a spiral staircase carpeted in orange. I struggle up the stairs behind it. The Lion of Bangor precedes me on the staircase, turning handles and opening doors. I try to do the same. In vain. The doors are rusted shut. Such a struggle with the doors, but not a sound. The air is burning and I have shooting pains in my head. Father, oh, my Father, take pity on your children. Don't leave the doors closed forever. Each of us, man by man, woman by woman, is indispensable. Look at us. We are no longer simply flesh. We are no longer simply wild beasts. We want to live in another place, like the birds, like the stars.

Night. The Eternal.

The Lion of Bangor is at his daughter's bedside. I am standing in the doorway. I am unobtrusive. I am a coward. I am terribly afraid of coming close to Noria's death. Of entering into her death. Death is awesome and imperial; we cannot keep it waiting and it does not permit itself to be hastened.

He has opened his bag—discoloured fabric over a rectangular framework which looks like a cardboard box—a poor sort of doctor's bag for a poor person's death. He is taking something out . . . they look like little yellow-orange globes . . . and now he is replacing all the light bulbs in the room with these bulbs. The Waiting Room becomes orange . . . a gentle, vegetable light. I see a meadow covered with wild flowers—tiger lilies, orange hawkweed, impatience, and buttercups.

The high white ceiling of the room now appears different—it hovers over the bed at the same time as the father hovers over his child. A space capsule. A journey through childhood prairies. Golden bough, rosy winds, sapphire, sidereal zephyr. I see him lightly pressing on Noria's jugular vein, pressing on certain nerves near her head. He is murmuring something. He is talking to her in a low voice. I am making an effort not to faint. I tiptoe out of the capsule. Later, he rejoins me.

"What are you thinking about?" he asks.

"I am thinking about the colour orange."

"That's the colour of the floor in your work room. I noticed it," he adds in a voice as soft as silk.

"I had never even thought about it," I say, disturbed despite myself.

"That yellow-orange colour must enlighten your mind."

"It is one of the colours of the dawn which sets fire to my heart!"

"In the last hours of life, orange light in the room makes it easier to focus one's mind," the Lion of Bangor says in a voice trembling with emotion.

"But why do you want her to concentrate!" I shout. "After all, it's a routine journey through congested streets and avenues."

"A routine journey? It's amazing how the minds of the living view death."

"You've put in these orange lights because you know that any chance of her recovering is decidedly remote, isn't that so?"

"What are you feeling, Jeanne?"

"I am feeling an enormous sadness for Noria and for you and for every human being who must clear so many obstacles in a battle whose outcome is known in advance. We are so afraid of going to Hell, we are so afraid of nothingness, of oblivion . . ."

"Hell! Oblivion! Where we are not wanted. After all, perhaps we are not required to go to Hell."

"I would do anything at all to avoid going to Hell. Oh, the seductive, desolate charm of lost causes . . ."

"So, at the moment of death, all one has to do is change direction, choose a different runway to take off from."

"The airplane crashed on takeoff. The pilot and the passenger perished."

"That doesn't get us anywhere. The plane rose in the air," the Lion of Bangor says, "It climbed and climbed, gliding over a mountain range coppery in the sunlight, a sea of strange radiance, to pierce the clouds and encounter subtle energies."

"If only this were true," I say, slightly dizzy from the takeoff, "if this were only true . . . Is it possible that nothing has been understood and nothing said by the living about death?"

"Of course it is possible. I am convinced that the evidence will soon emerge and we shall be granted tangible proof."

"A thought so vast and consoling that the dead will tremble and living women and men will fall to their knees from the impact of that lightning bolt?"

"Yes, it is possible," he says, smiling gently.

I have an image of Egypt, of a solar king near a canal and a golden barque, raising his hands and weeping as rain and death fall upon his child's body. I also hear Noria's words on the subject of her father. *"I was only a few hours old when he bent over me with his intense smile. First I was curious. Then I was afraid that this beast with his energy would absorb me and I screamed. I howled! There is nothing like that feeling of loneliness which we experience at the moment we are born on earth."*

"What are you doing with your life?"

He is getting up unsteadily, wavering on his long legs. The shadows of the night have made black holes where his eyes should be. Those loving thoughts about fathers, which I have never had, come easily to me when I look at the Lion of Bangor. But more than that, I feel something in me bowing in homage to their gifts and their luminous memory.

"Once upon a time," he is saying in a trembling voice, "a woman who led me to the regions of the dead asked me the same question, Jeanne."

"And what was your answer?"

"I said that I had crept into the funeral procession between the rot and the roses. We got married."

"Noria said that it was not a good marriage."

"I was good at making things difficult. I was possessed by a terrible demon."

"The one which cruelly insists on revealing the differences between men and women?"

"That one was never quite real to me. There is another one, very knowing, very destructive, which loves to throw oil on the fire of analogies, making them unbearable. When two genuinely creative and ambitious people, working full-time on projects which are essential to them, unite in marriage, it can give rise to an intensity which is difficult to maintain. When I read her inspired articles, her reports in the American or French journals, I often had the impression that she was drawing her best ideas from my own being and from the strength which animated my life. I would get up and hide myself at night to read her manuscripts. Every word sang its little song of erosion. Every sentence proclaimed the end of our life as a couple. She was going beyond me," he says, slumping down. "The woman I loved was large enough to give birth to a legend and I was shot through with jealousy and envy like an acid."

"But what did she blame you for?"

"She said that of the two of us, I was the more productive, that in my cancer research laboratory I was closer to grand desires and cosmic forces, and that the happiness I found there lit up my face. Even if we were both tortured by the decline and fall of the human race, it was ambition which ruled us both—the ambition to be the first, the innovators, to enlighten the world.

"We made each other suffer to the point that suffering became a mortal illness," he adds, and closes his eyes.

"What about the Spad? That whole aerial adventure?" I say with a tremor of impatience in my voice because I want to bury myself with Noria, and with her mother, in the depths of the sky.

"The plane? That was where all the harm I did came from. That was where I should have had the boldness and generosity to involve my life with that of the woman I loved, but instead I exhausted myself contemplating revenge and pitying myself for my fate," he says, his voice muffled.

I see the past attaching itself to him. He is not weeping. He is holding firm, steady on his feet.

"The plane, by some miracle, escaped the creditors of my father's financial empire. Half-covered by a tarp, it stayed at the end of a field which surrounded our house. The angel or devil of fate pretended to have forgotten it by the edge of a ditch. Every morning I saw my wife, with Noria in her arms, go to the window. She looked at the Spad the same way you look at a wild animal you do not dare tame and which makes your heart leap up. Witnessing this scene of silent contemplation, day after day, gave me goose flesh. Finally, worn out, but grudgingly, I shouted, 'All right, it's yours. I'm giving it to you. But I hope this plane will never separate us,' I added with a terrible foreboding. There was a humming in my ears when she turned her joy-filled face to me. Her physical presence, her body, even at a distance, overwhelmed me and I was always staggered by her approach. She came to kiss me. Her lips on mine made an enormous crevasse in the times of our life together," the Lion of Bangor says, closing his eyes, bowing his head as if the pain attached to this moment was still embodied in a fleeting scene.

The Lion of Bangor is sitting with his long legs crossed on the living room floor. At my feet, the two dogs are asleep, making little uneasy sounds. In Noria's room, the yellow-orange lights continue to keep watch, occasionally emitting an imperceptible crackling sound. They are starting to dim!

"With our child in her arms, this woman shot outside toward the thing which would return her to the world. Shot, Jeanne, shot! At that moment, I understood that this woman was an arrow. That was a revelation and there I stayed, in the grip of the exact clarity of that image," he says, raising his head to look at me.

"An arrow, a yearning, an energy set in motion . . ."

"A struggle, a fierce competition," he says, becoming indignant.

"In any case, you can't accuse her of lacking direction. On the contrary, the arrow intensifies direction," I say, becoming indignant in return.

"She always shot forward, protected by her aura and her extraordinary flood of personal charm," he says, in a hard and dry voice.

"You're not fair! Like her daughter, she was always alone, in the most touching way, without ever trying to hide it."

"She was an heiress, that's what she was."

"What inheritance are you talking about, for heaven's sake!"

"She inherited that terrible lack of understanding, the terrible situation between men and women. Just like the rest of us," he adds, his voice rising from his heart.

I see his face change, take on the face of a child, thin as paper, burnt in places. I see him raise his long arms to hide that flayed face in his hands. He is crying. His tears run toward his mouth. He is foundering in a sea of tears which is mounting, mounting in tides of despair. I shudder to see a man like that from the inside. Then, he tears himself away and looks at me with the expression of one who is inside the width of an incomparable space the dimensions of which are our terrestrial lives.

"Lion of Bangor, of whom, of what are we your children the heirs?"

"You, Jeanne, and all the men and women of your generation are the heirs of change. You will invent and imagine new connections between women, men, and all the kingdoms of the earth."

It takes an incredible effort for me to remain seated, not to rush at this very moment into his arms. A second later, it is too late; his expression has changed. Now he has the look of a castaway . . . .

"She was quickly in the air, for she was an arrow. She was finished with the plains of the earth. My teeth chattered. I reproached her with abandoning me, with taking pointless risks, with staying far too long in the air and of playing with her health.

" 'It is by force of circumstances,' my wife said. 'There are peculiar qualities in me which I did not know about.'

" 'And what do these peculiarities pertain to?' I asked her, trying to contain my fury.

" 'I believe they pertain to the sky and the clouds. I hear nothing in the great music you so love to listen to,' she said, clasping my hands, 'but when I hear the propeller's music, then I understand the best musicians better.'

"'I was happy before you came,' I told her, taking her head in my hands. 'For the first time in my life, I curled up at the feet of a woman because she was the most shining thing under the sun that I had ever seen. I loved it so much when we would come to a stop at night, to stretch out beside one another with our entire being.'

"'Whatever happens,' she interrupted, 'if ever I sleep next to a man again, it will be next to you.'"

What is the Lion of Bangor dreaming about? He is the object of an inrush of contradictory thoughts and feelings. All this happened a long time ago. But he sees it still and hears his wife's voice.

"That's how I learned . . ."

"I can't believe . . ." I say.

"I am speaking only the simple truth."

"However there is nothing more complicated than the truth."

"True enough," says the Lion of Bangor. "It is always necessary to defend the truth."

"And take the time to explain it . . ."

"Time? But I was in a terrible hurry," he says. "I did not want to take the time to sort out the part of me that cried out for revenge from the part that cried, *Come back, my love, you are part of my blood, and the strength which sustains me.* If you knew how loud vengeance called, Jeanne. Moaning, she danced her dance of death around me. In a matter of a couple of weeks, I passed from being an honourable and admired man to a public figure of fun. The need for revenge which possessed me found something to feed on every hour of the day. The mocking smiles. My enemies' triumphant attitude. The hypocritical compassion of other people. I am a doctor, a research scientist, I told myself, and everything that happens to me is subject to public criticism. But that could never justify all the evil which I did," he adds, bowing his head.

"Who was the other one? Who was your rival?"

"Harriet! She was a woman of independent means. She was a woman who flew, who became intoxicated by the skies. At that time, the spotlight was on her. Her name was on every lip and her daredevil reputation was growing every day. Everybody in Bangor knew that my wife was in love with her and probably sleeping with her. One day, at an air meet, they combined the flight paths of their airplanes to triumph over all the other competitors. That night, in a kind of stupor which was weighing me down, I looked at myself in the mirror to discover if I was still alive or if I already belonged to the infinite world of dreams. In the mirror I saw a man who wanted to bring them down in full flight. And the more I looked at myself, the more I learned things about this repulsive animal which lived within me.

"I had been contemplating this apparition for I don't know how long when I became aware of the creaking of wood and the shuffling of footsteps in my office. I went silently to the door, which was closed. I was too ill and too cold to speak or even to open that door. It was she who opened the door, she, Harriet. At that moment, something invisible seized hold of me. That thing was as heavy as lead and had the nauseating odour of ether. I looked at Harriet with her close-cropped skull and her eyes filled with a silent, burning thought. There was a rather frightening contrast between this vibration-filled head and that body which seemed inert, almost abandoned, as if she had withdrawn from herself.

"'You're right, I am already cut off from the living,' she told me in a voice muffled by pain. 'That gives us something in common, doesn't it?'

"'Get out of here,' I shouted, raising my arm to push her back.

"'I've come to show you something,' she said, quickly pulling open her long coat which was covering her legs. 'My doctor, a cautious man, is talking about a cellular transformation. And what do you, the great scientist, think?'

"'I think this is the greatest day of my life,' I told her, chortling. 'There is nothing else I can say to you. I hate you!'

"She didn't budge and gave me a contemptuous look.

"'Be a good loser,' she said to me in a silky whisper, 'for you have lost.'

"'No, you're the one who has lost. Pretty soon you'll be between four planks of wood. Or maybe you prefer cremation?'

"'You know, there's not a great deal of the original left to burn. They've just put a metal plate in my head, I have two more in my tibiae and I don't know how many of my ribs are made of silver.'

"'My diagnosis is certain,' I told her, pointing at her swollen legs. Certain kinds of cancer surface in areas which have received repeated traumas or in the region of a burn scar or chronic ulcer. This kind of cancer often takes the form of the object which caused the irritation.'

" 'We are leaving for Atlanta tomorrow,' she interrupted me.

" 'I doubt that radiation treatment can cure you.'

" 'Everything has been tried. I've been bombarded for weeks with alpha, beta, gamma rays. My cells are resistant to radiation.'

" 'So it is too late!'

" 'Too late? Flying up there, the faster you go the lighter time gets. It is as though it turns itself inside out,' she said, lighting a cigarette. 'Time becomes you. Your veins swell and all this overexcitement brings about a spectacular enchantment.'

" 'In the coming weeks, you'll need massive doses of enchantment and of time,' I told her.

" 'We're leaving for Atlanta tomorrow.'

" 'You already told me that! I hate that part of the country with all its violence and the vanity of those who want to remain pure.'

" 'We'll be staying with my friend, Mary Lane. She is a judge, the only woman judge in Atlanta. Her name is in the phone book. If you want to get in touch with your wife sometime.'

" 'What about my daughter, my little girl?'

" 'She's going with us. She's a baby. What would you do with a baby?' she asked me with genuine softness.

"She made a gesture of farewell. She was sparkling. I forced a smile as if what I was about to say had no importance at all.

" 'Tell my wife that I'm going to seize the Spad!'

" 'The Spad is parked in a hangar at the Bangor airfield. We're going in my plane.'

"Even though I felt I was on the road to ruin, I couldn't keep from adding, 'I'm going to ask for a divorce. She will get nothing. Nothing at all.'

" 'She doesn't want anything from you,' she told me.

" 'I can hear such terrible words inside myself.'

" 'If they are always so murderous, keep them to yourself,' she said, lowering her gaze to her legs.

" 'I have a clear mind.'

" 'And the feeling of having lost face!'

" 'You're completely without feelings,' I said. 'You've taken my wife, turned her against me, and jeopardized my reputation and my career.'

" 'Your career? You're a poor doctor, a doctor with neither heart nor soul. All you think about is your reputation and your honour,' she said, her breast heaving with her rapid breathing.

" 'Shut your dirty cancerous mouth!' I shouted straight in her face.

"Then everything became very confused. I could not contain my rage and I was hitting her on her chest and arms.

"When I finally stopped, shaking and sobbing, she was still looking at me, though her eyes were far, far away.

" 'Go on, get out of here!'

" 'You'll pay for this,' she said in a muffled voice.

"She left, dragging her steps as if she had chains on her ankles.

"I spent the rest of the night in fear of the day which was to come," the Lion of Bangor says. "I was awake. Then I slept and woke with a start. I dreamt that I was taking part in a disturbing ceremony along with hooded men and women. In this dream, one of these women handed me a torch and ordered me to light a large wooden cross on a mountain top above Atlanta. While the cross flamed red in the night, we all swore to keep a watchful eye on women's purity, to support patriotism and to maintain the supremacy of the white race."

"That sounds like a Ku Klux Klan nightmare," I say, shuddering.

"Yes, Jeanne. The Klan in all its horror."

"Where did this dream come from? Of course, Harriet had mentioned Atlanta."

"*Atlanta, we'll stay with my friend Mary Lane* . . ."

"The only woman judge in Atlanta."

"Judge and sovereign of the Klan empire! It was generally known in the freedom movement that it was Mary Lane who had unleashed the night raids. Mastered by my thirst for revenge, I had dredged up her name from the deepest depths of my mind . . ."

"What did you do?"

"I leapt in my car and drove to the airport. As I was driving along Bangor's Main Street, still sleeping under the leafy trees, I told myself that I was ready to forgive everything, to erase it all from my memory. Everything! Everything! Just so long as my wife and my little girl would not eat at the same table as the sovereign of the Ku Klux Klan.

"But since that damned car was neither quick nor powerful, when I got to the airfield, a little biplane was already on the runway. A breeze was blowing over the dust and dispersing a scent of magnolias. We don't have very many magnolias in New England, but I have always like their smell. At the end of the runway, Harriet's plane gathered speed and took off. Too late! All I could do was turn around and go home. I felt a weight against my left arm. You know, as if a little child had snuggled up against your chest and you were carrying it on your left arm because it is so light. An hour earlier I had been plunged in despair. And now here I was, ready to leave that very moment for Atlanta with the determination to wrest my wife and daughter from Harriet and the sovereign of the Klan.

"I slowed up a little trying to remember a period when I was capable of the most extraordinary feats of physical prowess. A period when I could treat fatigue, fear, and danger with total contempt. Oh, how much I would have liked to recover that unconscious physical vigour, that mythic vision of my youth. I was more than a man in his thirties whose beginning, middle, and end were inescapable. No! I was the Lion of Bangor, a husband, a father, and a burning force falling from heaven to the earth.

"In the air, the biplane was gaining altitude. It must have been around three hundred metres up and I was about to turn around when I saw two human forms leaping, bounding into space. They had been ripped from their seats by what must have been a terrible turbulence above. In that period, no one had thought to install seat belts. No one wore protective helmets. I saw two human bodies falling like parcels. The biplane continued its course through the blue sky before going into a nose-dive with kind of constant roaring noise. Do I still hear the sound of the bodies hitting the ground, biting the dust, when I close my eyes? A long animal scream, the sound of the explosion, the mocking song of a siren.

"I opened the car door, went a few steps, and fell to my knees on the ground. I addressed Someone whom I had not spoken to for a long time. How dare I! I invited him to take me on. Bare fists, a real fight, body against body, bloody, stopping only when exhausted. Poor, wretched humanity. Take pity, for once, take pity. Let me follow her around the world, to another world. However cruel my rage was against her, you know how much I love her. She, who is so much like me. My strange support.

"When I regained consciousness, I thought I was in the wrong time and the wrong place and that the discrepancy had been fatal. I seemed to see all the events of my life rolling toward me like rootless plants. I struggled with an uncontrollable nausea and I tried with all my willpower to go back into my coma. But someone stopped me. Someone was calling to me, shaking me. *Come back*, the voice was saying, *I beg you, come back . . . take one step . . . now the next one . . .* I opened my eyes—there in front of me was my wife's haggard face. I heaved my body up to throw myself into her arms and clasp her to me. I will never be able to have enough, I thought. But my wife freed herself. In a choking voice she kept repeating my rival's name. My courage failed me. 'Where is my daughter?' I asked, trying to control the panic which threatened to overcome me. She waved in the direction of the hangars—'over there.' I made her get in the car . . . I made a U-turn to avoid the scene of the catastrophe and drove toward the hangars—there, under the wings of my Spad, lying in a big willow basket, my daughter lay fast asleep and dreaming. They had been about to board that morning when a man who seemed to be in a hurry showed up—he wanted to make his first flight and right away. He was ashamed of having waited so long since he had been feeling a pull in himself toward the heights for a very long time.

" 'We're just about to take off,' Harriet had told him.

" 'I want to do it so badly. My friends tell me that you can get rid of all your fear and weakness in the air.'

" 'There are bad air currents today,' Harriet said, surprised and annoyed at his insistence.

" 'You'll have my eternal gratitude and a hundred dollars,' he said, almost crying.

" 'That's a good way of nipping resistance in the bud!'

" 'It's a peaceful way.'

"They boarded the plane. Harriet had, so it seemed, looked back at my wife. She smiled. They took off on the wings of death.

"At home, my wife and I had hardly closed the door when we let loose a dreadful symphony of accusations and reproaches. Tears, shouting, choking . . . Mouth wide open to deliver its destructive solo . . . another blow . . . did you fall? Will you finally fall? On your knees in the dust. You are an assassin, the score sang in funereal tones.

A useless fly looking for its body. Harriet had told her everything. My cynicism, my brutality, my threats. The keeper of the tomb. I opened and shut the doors as I pleased. My time would come to go under, to slide down the chute of death, shaking and beating my wings. I made a last effort to save myself and to save her," the Lion of Bangor says, "I wanted to make love with her. At that very moment! 'I'll give in to you from pity. I will always give in to you out of pity,' she added.

"She left the room to take refuge in the bathroom. I could hear the water running and I imagined her under the shower; it seemed to me that she was washing away her stains and I saw myself streaming off. I felt myself mix with the earth, becoming mud, becoming sludge. I was sitting in an armchair with my skin contracted from the cold. Under the shower, Harriet was laughing with her between life and death. Happy, freed, she was stroking her stomach, consoling and consoled. A bell tolled in my head, the stimulation of revenge reappeared, shamefully. In an epic, vengeance breathed in my ear, the strength and influence of heroes were measured by the size of the tests they had to overcome. Each new test presented fierce resistance. The larger the heroes grew, the more the obstacles appeared insurmountable. But they grew large enough to escape them. To all those who were observing from the outside and hoping for their fall, the heroes appeared to be going down, to be rolling in the mud, even while they were actually passing through and forging their fate at last.

"I got up to go. If for ordinary mortals, revenge is like a cold meal, for genuine heroes, it is a duty—the duty to retaliate, to defend themselves against the darkness which deals out counterblows to make them stumble once again.

At the morgue, the bodies of Harriet and the man were resting side by side. From their broken arms and contorted legs, it looked as if a grenade had blown them up from the inside. Harriet's cheekbones were crushed and a large bruise marbled her skull.

" 'Are you here for the autopsy?' the morgue attendant wanted to know.

"'No,' I said, 'one of my colleagues will be doing it. I knew one of the victims.'

"'In that case, I'll leave you alone. I'm having my lunch.'

"He left, humming a tune that was popular at the time and his song made a dozen vultures appear and gather at the end of the room. The morgue attendant did not seem to notice.

"I stayed there for quite a while. The spectacle of this formidable woman's corpse seemed to me a most reassuring object. Harriet—an angel of fire, a pure daughter of the earth? Twenty-four hours earlier, this pitiful creature who was stretched out on a slab in the morgue had been a dangerous beast in my kingdom. I bent over her corpse. Now and then, I chattered my teeth in the direction of the vultures who were observing me, to remind them that this prey belonged to me.

"A few hours later, I was back home and shut in my laboratory. My wife and daughter were asleep. I worked all night long, crazed with revenge, crazed with love. A closed-off man, completely insensible to the outside world. Early in the morning I went to wake my wife. Her cheeks were wet.

"'I have something to show you,' I told her calmly.

"She looked at me suspiciously but my expression must have reassured her more or less since I had adopted the look and tone of a man who had been working in his workshop and who was proud of his work. She got up and followed me to the lab.

"'See,' I said, 'the remarkable results of a single night of effort.'

"She took a deep, deep breath, trying to relax the contraction which was gripping her chest.

"'I have been working all night to develop a new cell culture and I have been successful!'

"'Where did the original cells come from?' she asked in a voice in which fear was digging a pit.

"'From the Bangor morgue. I took some cells from that woman whose loss is causing you such an exaggerated sorrow. I've even given a name to these cells—HAR cells. From now on, I'm going to devote my time to distributing these cells to every research laboratory in America. That way, Harriet will continue her cellular life in perpetual growth.'

"She drew back. She looked at me with an expression filled with horror.

" 'A monstrous growth!' she said, almost nauseated.

" 'I have redirected death,' I said, and felt a sticky sort of pain rising in me.

" 'You are an evil spirit. Oh, good God, why have you done this thing? Why?'

"Her voice was so broken. She was grieving with her whole soul. To try to relieve her distress, I went toward her, my arms outstretched. She pushed them away as though I had torrents of blood dripping from the ends of my fingers. Something rose in my throat.

" 'I am going to leave you.'

" 'You will always be my love,' I told her and wept.

" 'Don't try to stop me. It's useless. I am leaving with my daughter. We have the right to escape the sewers where our life is lost. As far as revenge goes, you are a master of it. What I wish for you,' she added in a murmur, 'is that this hatred you feel for Harriet will be lifted from you. Human beings have no right to vengeance!'

"After my wife and little girl left, in a fit of shame, I eliminated the HAR cells from the face of the earth. But it was too late . . . Harriet was alive in me, breathing the air I breathed. She was with me wherever I went. There she was, when I was hunting, about to shoot partridges and quail, or fishing, or even in the whorehouse. When I slept, she pressed close to me until I almost suffocated. I awoke gasping for breath—had they slept together? Had they made love to the point of ecstasy, slowly, marvelling at the heat of passion coursing through their bodies?

"When I asked these questions, my thoughts always ended by stopping by the edge of a little dusty road at the bottom of a ravine. I would get out of the car, see the silhouette of my enemy standing out against a dark sky. Harriet would look at me without trembling, without begging, and I would coldly butcher her with my carbine. I would throw her corpse in the bushes and hope that every carrion-eater would pass through by day and by night.

"During the years after my wife and daughter left, I lived with shame and with revenge, Jeanne. When I had had enough, I stuffed myself with pills and alcohol. When my pain was at its height, I preferred to think about my wife's inability to remain in one place, about her ambitions to be a pilot, a daredevil, a feminist, and a caretaker of the dead. And about her fascination, her indecent, sweat-soiled passion for another woman. There it was—the cause of all the harm! That's what had destroyed our marriage. In this whole damned story, wasn't I the sacrificial lamb? A lamb who had been forced somehow to wear wolf's clothing to fulfill a just mission of rage. And the wolf had buried his white teeth into the heart of the flesh. A kind of ill-defined oppression kept me from coming to terms with the truth," the Lion of Bangor says, dropping his head heavily into his hands. "I needed time, too much time, to recognize my cruelty and my responsibility."

"During all those years, my wife never made the slightest contact. Not a single letter. Now and then in the newspapers I read, I saw her life—a crisscross of flying exhibitions and air meets. Every time I read her name, I felt ill. I saw her beautiful, desirable face once more and I understood what a terrible thing this separation was. But I never tried to see her again, not even in a roundabout way. I was waiting for a profound and incomparably intimate peace to creep into me. Doing penance, I summoned this peace. I also did penance with the aim of purging myself of all the harm I had inflicted on my wife and on Harriet, because I was haunted, literally haunted, by the torments I had perpetrated on Harriet after her death. Something told me that a human being has no right to pursue his revenge on a dead person. Wherever she was, Harriet could have seen the repugnance I felt for her. And she suffered from it.

"I believe with all my heart and with something larger than my intelligence and reason, that long ago, humans had a clear-sighted vision of the dead. After our dead passed on, we could follow their ascent and their journey by paying them infinite homage. We recognized our dead and their presence was dear."

"What is the effect of the hatred of the living on a dead person?"

"Jeanne," he says, "hatred paralyses them. It keeps them on earth. Our hatred exhausts them and puts barriers in the way of their best intentions."

"What happened when you stopped loathing Harriet?"

"I stopped being ashamed. I stopped being faithful to those cruel, vengeful, and destructive characters whom I incarnated or who incarnated themselves in me. I was convinced in myself that the day would come when, purged of my gross and possessive nature, I could appear before my wife and child without shame and without remorse."

"And did that day come?"

"It never did. It gave up the ghost with all the energy of ignorance the day my wife nose-dived into a concrete pylon supporting some high cables. The final embrace of matter and fate."

"And in what sky was this?"

"You are very sharp, Jeanne—in the sky over Atlanta. I learned the news from a newspaper which was a few days old. This paper is mistaken, I shouted and tore it into pieces. Little by little I felt the heat of a hellish fire pervade me. I left immediately for Atlanta. It seemed to me that I drove for an eternity, maddened by the thought that I would never see her, that I would never touch her again. I would dig a great hole under the pines or cedars where I would lie down with her. I would shut myself up in the coffin where they had laid her.

"Her remains had already been buried in the old Atlanta cemetery. A small grey tombstone. Freshly turned earth. Reality. I was on my knees.

"Later, when I raised my head, I saw someone looking at me from a distance. It was a stone angel, upright on a cement pedestal, standing in the brilliant light of the middle of the autumn morning. Behind it stretched a row of magnolia trees in which the birds were singing as loud as they could. Everything was calm within the bluish shadow of nature. The autumn leaves were slowly falling everywhere. I looked at this angel who knew all these graves and all these dead. It had remained here for ages like this, upright between the earth and sky. How it drew me, sucked me toward it. Perhaps stone angels attract the birds as well as wandering and desolated spirits.

"Going closer, I noticed that a vine had attached its tendrils to the pedestal and the angel's contours. In growing, they had closed in on the angel in a kind of vegetable embrace, as if they wanted to keep it on the earth. For the first time in my life, I was in the presence of an angel. In the old Atlanta cemetery, this stone angel extended one hand toward the blue sky in a way both delicate and vulnerable, while the other seemed to plunge deeply into the earth that held the dead.

"I stayed a long time in front of the angel. I waited. I listened. Ear to ear, heart to heart, a voice with my wife's inflections breathed to me that I was before the Angel of the Presence and that its power had entered my life. *It stands in the eternal light where love and will are one.* Then the voice which spoke to me changed its inflection. *It is like you and you are like It,* a voice which sounded like Harriet's whispered. A cry arose which came from the depths of my being. 'My daughter! Give me back my daughter. We are made of the same substance. The blood relationship is sacred!'

"Show me the road, I asked, crying real tears both visible and invisible. *Knee to knee, toe to toe, you will advance with the Angel of the Presence along every road,* Harriet's voice whispered to me. *Every path is illuminated,* my wife's voice whispered for the last time."

The Lion of Bangor closes his eyes. He remains silent. His face is at once beautiful and melancholy. He moves a little, turning his gaze toward the window. The snow is falling heavily. Soon it will be day. Is he about to rise and give himself over to his daughter? Will he cut the immediate contact now between us? Moreover, I am not sure I can follow him into Noria's life. Am I about to have a vulgar argument with him, reproaching him for his violent changes of heart, his cruelty? I am afraid of allowing myself to fall into the trap of an unaccustomed softness.

"I followed every road," he says, finally.

"Was Mary Lane's the first?"

"Yes, but she wasn't there. 'A study trip,' a hostile secretary told me and slammed the door in my face. Then I followed the courthouse route, up the stairways of lawyers, civil servants, police, and clergymen. They made me wait behind their doors. I retraced my steps hundreds and hundreds of times, like a mouse in a maze. Everyone in Atlanta knew me after a month. The madman rambling on about his daughter who has disappeared. There were many questions, too many questions. At the hotel I was staying in, the phone woke me often at night.

"They suggested I leave the city immediately. I received threats of death and destruction. My house in Bangor would be set on fire! For several days I was prey to a dark terror. But I would not give up! I took another route and hired a private detective to whom I told the whole story for the hundredth time. Did he listen to me? He repeated my story without leaving out a single detail, taking into account my subsequent corrections. I felt he was careful to present my story as I wanted it to be. Then he added a few details that were not my own. He brought the picture to life by bringing in, little by little, the invisible empire of the Klan with its Imperial Wizard, assisted by its Grand Cyclops, Grand Dragons, Hydras, and the other night-riders."

" 'You tell me that your daughter has blonde hair and blue eyes, and that her mother was neither Jewish nor Catholic, trade unionist nor immigrant. So, we may have a chance to get her back.'

" 'For God's sake, what have they done with her?'

" 'It's what the women have done with her,' he corrected. 'It's the Klanswomen who are concerned with the children and who make all the decisions. You know there are as many women as men in the Ku Klux Klan. The members of the Klan are divided into three more or less equal parts—one-third children, one-third adults, and one-third old people.'

" 'What power do the women have?'

" 'Does Stone Mountain mean anything to you?'

" 'It is a sinister monument,' I said.

" 'Carved out of the live rock, it is a sculpture in high relief which represents a cavalcade of Confederate generals, with Robert E. Lee at their head, ordered in its entirety by the United Daughters of the Confederacy, one of the numerous Klan associations. It is the rallying point for all the Klans in North America. It is probably one of the oldest American secret societies.'

" 'You know a lot about it.'

" 'I am absolutely obsessed by it,' he told me seriously. 'When I was a teenager, I saw a black servant I was fond of taken in the dead of night by hooded, torch-wielding people. A plump hand with red nails applied a big .45 to my dear Sarah's forehead. I swear that the woman's hand did not shake at all as she delivered Sarah to her death. When I wanted to intervene, they knocked me to the ground with their rifle butts.'

" 'Where does the name come from?' I asked him after a moment of silence.

" 'Some people pretend that *Klux* is a variation on *Lux*, light. But they also say that the Greek word *Kuklos*, a circle, is the source. They also say that it's a kind of imitation of the sound of someone shooting off his rifle. For myself, I am convinced that the three *K*'s are the initials of Kill! Kill! Kill!'

" 'You are putting your life in danger for me and my daughter,' I told him.

" 'I'm a little crazier and a little more reckless than some others.'

" 'I believed that all detectives were men who did not fool around, who were cautious about everything and who thought all stories were by definition packs of lies which they had to open up to the light of day.'

" 'And I thought that doctors were cold men, gripped by the conviction that ultimately death would fix everything up.'

" 'Do you try to find out what the individuals who come to see you really want?'

" 'I am convinced that, beyond what they are pleased to tell me, there is a more secret, more cruel reality which they try to keep from me.'

" 'I didn't want to fool you. I've told you all the essentials.'

" 'I believe you,' he said and got up to walk me to the door. He had a limp.

" 'You should go back to Bangor. Atlanta should forget you.'

" 'I've set off the alarms. I've probably made your task unnecessarily complicated.'

" 'At another time, I would have said yes. But now, Hitler is our protection. His spectacular successes in Europe are getting the Klan worked up. After all, they are precursors of Naziism. They feel as if they are living in an adventure novel, some great epic of fascist propaganda. They howl and they bay, they are absolutely out of their minds. This is our chance. Be confident—the threads of destiny will be unravelled in the end,' he added, clasping my hand.

"Three years went by," the Lion of Bangor says. "My friend from Atlanta pursued his investigation with unshakeable confidence. 'Your daughter is alive. I feel it. I know it. We are getting closer to her. She is living her life somewhere else as a stolen child and she will always be somewhere else if we don't move. But we are ready to pounce and grab her at the slightest opportunity. Part of our America is territory occupied by the forces of evil. Wherever you turn—fear, servitude, incrimination. The Ku Klux Klan delights in mixing racism and kerosene to feed the torches they light in the mountains. But we are noticing that, every day, the tension, that powerful tension which up till now has been able to keep their forces together is weakening as Hitler's armies have already faltered. The Klan is staging its last night-rides and terror attacks. They are frightened as they have never been before. Soon they will be walking through the valley of tears. They will probably make a final effort to avoid breaking up, but they will not be able to long withstand the innate need for freedom and justice which burns within the citizens of this country and of the whole world. Even in the midst of our efforts to recover your daughter, my friends and I keep hearing a great invocation which is becoming more and more palpable and which bowls us over with its strength and intensity. It is the invocation to the spirit of liberation. It is the prayer of the human spirit for dignity. Do you hear it where you are?' he wrote me."

"Where were you, Lion of Bangor? Had you left America?"

"After the American landing in North Africa, I, along with everyone else, was plunged into the whirlpool of war. I was an army doctor in Tunisia and Sicily. My stubborn, faithful friend in Atlanta was right—there was something inexpressible in the air, a new, increasing point of tension which helped us to overcome the insurmountable difficulties on every front which had been erected in front of our soldiers and our armies. After the war, I went to Nuremberg. I remember. It was the fall of 1946. There was a telegram—*Daughter found. Come at once.*

"I went home immediately. I was grasped by a terrible anguish. I had to come to terms with my past and walk the length of a forgotten corridor of neglect and gloom. Alone, over the pitiful track of my vanity and pride. But now all the principle witnesses were dead, I could take refuge in innocence. What a temptation! I could have said that I had done nothing, even if that nothing had killed me a little. No! The garbage of my life is still my life.

"My friend was waiting for my at the airport, his face pale.

" 'I have a terrible feeling,' I said, clasping him in my arms.

" 'You have been through terrible battles,' he said.

" 'Where did you find her? Where is she?'

" 'We found her in a Brown Shirt camp of the American Fascist

Party. The party is destroyed so they are destroying their young people. The wolves are turning on their pups. They are no longer afraid of endangering themselves.'

" 'Where is she?'

" 'In a clinic. They have stolen her soul.'

" 'Don't be absurd!' I said, repressing an urge to throw up.

" 'She was held in a brothel for six months. She was provided to satisfy the fantasies of the young men in the German-American Bund and the Brown Shirts.'

" 'Why? Why?'

" 'Out of revenge. The Klan knows about her mother's lesbian history.'

" 'Did you?'

" 'I knew her. I knew Harriet.'

" 'I am astounded,' I said. 'I feel I am viewing the lengthy progress of destiny. Is it a cosmic progress? I see it triumphing, stage by stage, along the whole egocentric chain.'

" 'Harriet would have said the same thing! She had an astonishing comprehension of what is. I found each of her movements imprinted with an infinite grace. When I saw her sit down and light a cigarette all my emotions were fused. Each time, there was a moment of grace and a moment of distress . . .'

" 'You knew that she loved women.'

" 'She told me.'

" 'She rejected you?'

" 'Yes. She made a special effort so that I would not be permanently wounded by her refusal. She was ten years older than I. I was a romantic adolescent, trying to open my heart to the beauty of the world, to communication with those like me.'

" 'Harriet . . . the Klan . . . I assumed . . .'

" 'That poisonous fog made her sick. The Klan called her a nigger."

" 'But what about Mary Lane? Her friend Mary Lane?'

" 'She must have said that out of pure derision. To get back at you.'

" 'I have left a blasted field behind me,' I said.

" 'You have been abandoned. You have been left alone. But there will always be a new springtime in you, my friend.'

" 'Even when they have stolen your soul?' I asked, thinking of my daughter.

" 'Your daughter is still a fragment of the universe. Like you and me.'

" 'You haven't told me everything,' I cried, drawing myself up against the sky like a warrior ready to attack.

" 'Her body still bears the marks of a pregnancy. She had a baby in August, a little boy.'

" 'Where is he?'

" 'The Klanswomen who take care of adoptions took him without her even seeing him. But some people say your daughter killed him. Maybe they are happy to repeat what they have been told to say.'

" 'My daughter is not a murderer. But even if she were . . .'

" 'Come on,' he said, taking me to his car.

"I brought home a skeletal teenager with yellow skin, who had lost her identity," the Lion of Bangor says, grasping my hand very hard. Someone who has lost her identity is someone who was present at the death of the sun!"

"A particle, a drop of essential matter, a single breath," I say, "might have been enough to revive someone who has lost her soul."

"There is something presiding over the distribution of energies," he says. "I believe it is the devotion of one loving nature to another. Every day I willed that my strength should mix with my daughter's last strength. Eye to eye, we remained opposite each other. Heart to heart, breath to breath, I tried to inspire a new spirit in her."

"Did she talk about the past, or about the baby?"

"She often said to me, 'Daddy, I will know the whole truth about myself someday, because I am the only one with the power to speak it.' "

"And what did her medical records have to say?"

"Behind the mumbo-jumbo, her medical records all said the same thing—chronic depression and partial amnesia. They also said that she had tried twice to kill herself."

"And what did you say?"

"I said that my daughter was an astral madwoman and that I was prepared to give my life for her."

"An astral madwoman?"

"It is the midnight of the soul, Jeanne. She dragged her wings amidst the gloom. Held to the earth by her emotional nature, she slept among the dead, with no hope of return. Her soul foresaw that Pegasus, the winged horse of love, would never again carry her through the open sky. She will never fly in ecstasy with the great Eternal Swan. The fragile human condition. My daughter's hard psychic and personal shell began to melt during the night. Her memory returned and she began to relive fragmentary versions and visions of horror. Sleep dug into her memory, sent her back down to hell where she could follow that sewer to its source. Sometimes in the day time, she stopped living, letting out a feeble groan of a damned soul. I wished that death would come to end such an interlude."

"What did you do to prevent her from burying herself in insanity?"

"I tried to create an alternative universe for her, to force her in another direction . . ."

"Toward nature, toward animals . . ."

"I took her with me to the forests, to the mountains. I told her about the evolution of the earth and all its facets and metamorphoses. The ancient condition of the constellations and the history of the stars fascinated her."

"Knee to knee, toe to toe, like the time in the old Atlanta cemetery when the Angel of the Presence raised its hand to the blue sky," I say.

"We were facing each other on a trail. I was looking at my daughter and she recognized me. I saw her reborn and returning among us," the Lion of Bangor adds, after a long moment.

"And what about the child, and your wife, and Harriet?"

"Nothing was ever said until she became an adult."

"Why?"

"I was waiting until all the childhood castles had finished their resurrection."

"No," I say, "you were afraid and ashamed."

"I was overcome with pity," he interrupts. "Pity for her, pity for myself. She had the same golden hair as her mother, the same fracture in her smile after I had told her everything. She said nothing. Her silence made me feel that I had told her a tissue of lies."

" 'I've been wanting to know for a long time,' she said when I was finished.

"'Why didn't you ask me?'

"'Drive me to the bus station,' she said and rose.

"'Where are you going?' I asked, even though I knew the answer.

"'I have an appointment in Atlanta and I'm late already.'

"'Your son?'

"She closed her eyes and nodded her head slightly. She looked like an old and wounded spirit.

"'I don't want you to leave me,' I said, clasping her in my arms.

"'If you want to do something more for me, allow me to leave,' she said, disengaging herself.

"'If you want to do something for me, try always to love yourself a bit better. Do not erase the mark of the union between us,' I added, with some anguish.

"'I will always need you,' she said, looking indecisive and unhappy.

"'We have a friend in Atlanta.'

"I left her at the bus station. I waited a week before calling Atlanta.

"'Is my daughter with you?'

"'She's gone out to look around,' my Atlanta friend said.

"His voice sounded strange on the phone.

"'I sense some obstacles,' I said.

"'Your sonar is working well,' he answered.

"'What's wrong?'

"'Your daughter is a tiny little fish hunting sharks in the deepest waters.'

"'What is going on?'

"'She's got company,' he said with some hesitation.

"'Don't you trust me?'

"'It's my business not to trust people.'

"'But not me!'

"'No, not you. With you I can please myself.'

"'Who is with her?'

"'A guy,' he said. Someone from the old days . . . in the brothel. She recognized him. Last night she brought out the whole story in bursts. She met this guy in a bar. He told her all she wanted to hear.'

"'About her son?'

"'Yes. She's prepared to follow this guy to the end of the world.'

"'We must do something!'

"'We must tell her the truth.'

"'The truth?'

"'Her son is dead.'

"'Dead?'

"All at once I felt terribly tired, all my fighting spirit exhausted.

"'I should have warned you,' my friend from Atlanta said. 'It happened a long time ago.'

"'It couldn't have been as long ago as all that.' I said bitterly. 'My grandson would have been barely six years old.'

"'When I heard about it, I went to Bangor to tell you. I was driving slowly in the car, looking for your house. I came across you and your daughter. She was holding a large bunch of wild flowers in her arms. You had your arm around her shoulders. There were magnificently coloured clouds in the sky. Perhaps it was a strange way to express friendship,' he added after a short pause.

"'Not at all. That's the loveliest and most generous thing you've ever done for me and my daughter.'

"'Somebody is opening the door.'

"'Give her anything she asks for.'

"He hung up. There were tears in my eyes as if everything was over between my daughter and myself.

"Around midnight, the phone rang.

"'She's gone,' he said. 'I've just taken her to the airport. She asked me for a ticket to Los Angeles and a thousand dollars. She left a message for you. I can read it to you if you like.'

"'Don't bother.'

"'Her letter is full of contradictory feelings and sweeping statements. I believe that in leaving today she will turn toward the outside world. She is going to try to live with everything that comes from herself, from you, from her mother.'

"'My grandson . . . He . . .'

"'I am sorry, but I cannot tell you anything further. She made me promise.'

"I laughed bitterly.

"'I have lost everything. It is a curse!'

"'She will come back,' he said. 'One fine morning . . .'

"'Why must truth always lie on the opposite side of the chasm?' I asked.

" 'I have seen you leap the abyss,' he said.

" 'Next week, I will go back to the old cemetery in Atlanta and lay some flowers.'

" 'We'll go together. Harriet is buried in the same cemetery. She's at the end of a row . . .'

" 'Of magnolias, near an angel. She told me once . . .'

" 'I'll be waiting for you,' he said, with a strange emotion in his voice.

"Six months later, I got a letter from her," the Lion of Bangor says. "She was working nights in a bar and taking a pilot's course in the daytime. Fondly, Noria.

"There was no address on the envelope. Why had she bothered to write? I had long conversations with her. I interceded. I begged. Come back, little creature. We are but children. We are all children and we put our arms around those just like us. We are not perfect and we love what is imperfect, pitiful, and mortal.

"Soon it was summer, July, and the sun burned like fire. One fine morning . . . She seemed to have aged.

" 'Your arms are open so wide,' she said to me.

" 'It comes from my heart. Look,' I said, leading her to the bottom of the meadow which lay around our house.

" 'The Spad!'

"The look she gave me was ecstatic.

" 'I've had it made like new.'

" 'It is sleeping with its head tucked under its wing between two firmaments,' she said.

" 'In the name of your mother, of Harriet, and of all eternal voices, this is your plane.'

"My daughter was flying. It was so beautiful. Now and then a shadow marched across the windows of my workroom. I thought that she was rocking in her cradle up there. No, she was not going to take part in speed and endurance races around the world.

" 'I have made certain commitments in my conscience and my heart,' she told me one day. 'A protest is starting up in California against the torture of laboratory animals. I can do more. I can snatch the animals away from their torturers.'

" 'An underground action? Springing the locks?'

" 'Yes,' she told me. 'There is some risk . . .'

" 'I support you.'

" 'A new era of compassion wants to be born on earth.'

" 'I am an old beast. I've hunted, I've killed, but I know that there is a magnetic connection between the animals and ourselves.'

" 'They are the mirror image of what we are.'

"And that is how it all began," the Lion of Bangor says. "I kicked down doors and broke windows and locks to accomplish my daughter's will. We found allies, friends, havens and refuges. It was all comparatively simple for me, but for her—having to go back and forth, to turn in the sky. All those bloody paw prints in the Spad. You know the rest, Jeanne. Here I am with you, after fourteen years of waiting."

"Of waiting? What have you been waiting for? For pardon?"

"I've been waiting for her to share. I've been waiting for her to share her secret with me."

"The child's death, your grandson? That is a terrible secret. I should also like to know," I say. "I have been coming closer and closer to Noria's secret. As far as the Klan was concerned, what was one murder more or less in the world?" I say, casting my terrible fishing net over the old lion.

"But she kept it for fourteen years."

"What about you?"

"I've only known for a few months. One drop of water in an acid bath."

"Do you know all the circumstances surrounding the child's death?"

"He died after a series of immersions in water. It was a Pavlovian experiment very much in vogue at the end of the forties."

"A human guinea pig?"

"The Klan provided him to the researchers. One baby among so many others—they brought the mentally handicapped, orphans, and abandoned and rejected children as well. Creatures as powerless and defenceless as laboratory animals. The Klan was only one supplier among many others. So many others."

"Did your friend in Atlanta give you all these details?"

"What was that noise?"

All of sudden, the Lion of Bangor is restless, on the alert.

"It's nothing," I say. "It's the wind blowing through the branches of the maple tree above the roof."

"No," he says, "it is death."

He rushes toward Noria's room. At floor level, something is passing, raising a fine dust. The dogs are up, their muzzles in the air, their paws trembling. The Lion of Bangor is bending over his daughter. He is speaking to her, stroking her hands. I come closer. I am very far away. He invents a little girl playing high, high in the sky upon the Great Bear's breast, with a rainbow and some dogs to the music of the birds and propellers.

I ask Noria's forgiveness for having stolen her secret.

Later on, we order a pine coffin from the old guard.

"Embalming? Burial? She will certainly suffer," the old guard mutters.

"It is so I can take her with me. In Bangor I will have her body cremated. I promise you."

"Another wrench!" the old guard mourns.

"I will return in the springtime," he says. "We will scatter her ashes along the Appalachian trail."

We escort the Lion of Bangor and Noria to the border on ski-mobiles, the old guard and I. In force, just like the grandmothers who bend above the fires of the earth and sky to warm themselves.

The little plane is always at the pond's edge. It is as lovely as an epic which might have entered into our souls to draw closer to us. It is as lovely as a trusting thought.

Étang-aux-Oies
Autumn, 1985—Spring, 1987